Playing for Blood

By Chuck Anderson

PublishAmerica
Baltimore

ISBN: 1-60441-236-4 (softcover)
ISBN: 978-1-4489-6064-4 (hardcover)
PUBLISHED BY PUBLISHAMERICA, LLLP
www.publishamerica.com
Baltimore

Printed in the United States of America

Prologue

The small boat careened precariously, tossed about by the huge breakers that crashed on the beaches of a narrow stretch of land at the eastern end of Long Island, called Amagansett by the local natives. There were three people in the unsteady craft. Two of them, barefoot and dressed in tattered clothing held together by ropes knotted at the waist, strained at the long oars that somehow managed to propel the small boat towards the shore. They looked at the roiling waves with wild and fearful eyes, for even though they had been at sea for most of their lives, neither knew how to swim. The team of rowers was directed in its efforts by a bear of a man who sat at the stern, pulling the tiller and skillfully maneuvering the boat through the surf. He was dressed in grimy trousers, sea boots, and a silk shirt stained by sweat, blood, and gunpowder. His long, greasy black hair was tied back with a piece of leather. Two pistols and a short saber were tucked in his wide belt. At his feet, there was a small chest, ostensibly filled with trinkets to trade with the Indians for fish and fruit. After what seemed to be hours, the three seafarers wrestled the boat ashore and jumped into the knee-deep water, staggering as they regained their land legs. One of the seamen grumbled as he hoisted the chest to his shoulder and started trudging towards the sand dunes that formed a low ridge between the beach and the forest of pine and oak that covered most of the island before the arrival of woodcutters from Connecticut fifty years later. His partner stayed with the boat, looking about nervously for savages or strange beasts in this foreign land. The helmsman, who was also the captain of the swift, six-gun sloop anchored offshore, followed the chest-bearer, scanning the dunes carefully for hostile Indians. As the captain entered the forest, he looked for familiar markings to get his bearings, for he had been here before. As soon as he spotted a familiar cutlass slash on a tree, he directed the seaman to put down the chest. The seaman, used to the brutal and arbitrary orders of his captain, obeyed without question, but was puzzled when the captain pulled out a spade from its hiding place behind a giant oak tree and told him to start digging.

"But, Cap'n, I thought we was goin' to trade with—"

"Start diggin', matey, and no questions, if y' know what's good for ye."

The seaman started turning over the loamy earth, cursing under his breath. After the chest that obviously did not contain trinkets but objects of greater value was properly buried, the sweating seaman looked up, only to stare into the muzzle of one of the captain's pistols.

"Sorry, lad, can't have anyone know..." The last words the seaman heard were obliterated in a single, blinding flash.

Thus a certain Captain William Kidd, former Manhattan banker and social lion, added to the treasure buried near a giant oak on the shores of Long Island, treasure that would be lost for several centuries.

This was the treasure that many believed Kidd had buried on Gardiner's Island to the north, the treasure he had tried to use as a bargaining chip during his trial before an English court.

As it turns out, he was not the last visitor to this site. A few years later, in 1776, a schoolteacher from Connecticut was put ashore nearby. He changed into dry clothes near the giant oak, then set off to spy on the British forces that controlled the island. Unfortunately, he was caught and hanged, proving that he had but one life to give for his country.

Oh, we don't give a damn for our old Uncle Sam,
Way-o, whiskey and gin!

Lend us a hand when we stand in to land
Just give us time to run the rum in.

During Prohibition, an average of 10,000 cases of liquor a week found their way from beaches such as this on Long Island to the speakeasies of New York City. Affluent, college-educated gentlemen rumrunners, skilled in sailing and seamanship, enthusiastically joined forces with local fisherman to keep the steady stream of liquor flowing into New York, Connecticut, and New Jersey.

In the early 1920's, another kind of pirate, Black Jack Bouvier, accompanied by his Wall Street cronies and local landscapers, stood in the shade of the giant old oak and planned the layout of what was to become one of the most exclusive golf courses on Long Island.

In 1942, John Cullen, a 21-year-old Coast Guardsman, was starting his six-mile patrol of the Amagansett Beach. The stately oak that towered above a stand of scrub pine marking the edge of the exclusive Treasure Oak Country Club marked the beginning of his tour of duty. Night walks were particularly lonely for the Coast Guard "sand pounders"—windows on the beach houses were blacked out, and the beaches themselves were empty. Still thinking of the warm embrace of his girlfriend, Cullen barely noticed some shadows outlined in the night's darkness.

He thought, "Probably just some fishermen, but I'd better check anyway."

The man in the glare of Cullen's flashlight didn't look like a fisherman. Unlike most "Bonnackers," he was clean-shaven, dressed entirely in black, and spoke impeccable English, as if he had learned it in England. He explained that he and his companions had run aground and were waiting for the tide to change.

Cullen said, "But you must know the regulations. You're only supposed to fish in the daytime. You're going to have to come with me back to headquarters."

The would-be fisherman responded with an odd question, "How old are you?"

The Coast Guardsman frowned. "Twenty-one," he said. "What's that got to do with it?"

7

'You have a mother and a father? A girlfriend? Do you want to see them again?"

As the leader spoke, Cullen could see two of the men muttering to each other and moving behind him. One of them said something in response to the other. It didn't sound like English to Cullen.

The spokesman turned and hissed at the man, "Shut up, you fool!"

Cullen realized he was in danger. Armed with only a flare gun, he knew he had to think fast. Maybe dumb was the way to play it.

"What's in the bag, clams?" he asked, noticing one of the men dragging a bag across the sand.

The leader of the group moved closer. "You don't know what this is about," he said. He reached into his pocket and pulled out a wad of bills. "Take it," he said, thrusting over $200 into Cullen's hand. "Forget about this. Forget you ever saw us."

Cullen felt he had a choice: if he didn't take the money, they would shoot or stab him; if he took it and got out of this alive, he could show it to his chief as evidence. Carefully, he put the money in his pocket.

The leader pulled Cullen close and said, "Look at me. Would you recognize me if we met on the street in Southampton?"

"No," Cullen stammered.

He was released suddenly. As he backed slowly into the fog, he was sure someone would fire or come after him, but nothing happened. As the intruders turned into vague outlines, Cullen turned and ran, his boots sinking into the sand like lead weights. As if in a bad dream, Cullen ran for three miles. The only thing he heard was his rasping breath.

Later that night, Cullen, his chief of station, and six other Coast Guardsmen with rifles returned to search the area. They found nothing. They were about to give up and return to the station when they heard a sound out in the water and felt the beach vibrate. Hiding behind a sand dune, they looked into the early morning mist and saw the outline of a U-boat. Diesel engines grunted as the ghostly vessel worked itself off a sand bar and disappeared beneath the waves.

Later, as the Coast Guardsmen searched the beach for signs of the spies, Cullen spotted a pack of cigarettes. Next to it was a wet trail in the sand, as if something had been dragged. Following the trail for several yards, they found a rolled up pair of pants, and a three-foot square of wet sand. In minutes, they had uncovered four tin-covered boxes full of explosives and detonators, and a canvas bag containing German uniforms. One of the searchers said, "Well, it ain't Captain Kidd's lost treasure, but it will do for now."

Chapter 1

Stanley was dead.

I looked at the line in my journal and thought, "Jeez, I sound like Charles Dickens." I started the journal habit back in college, where I had an English teacher who made us keep journals for our entire freshman year. We had to react in writing to everything we read before we were allowed to talk about it in class. He used to say, at least once a week, "The unexamined life is not worth living." To me and about half the guys in the class, survivors from the Korean police action going to school on the GI bill, the notion of the unexamined life was not without some significance. About halfway through the first semester, I realized the professor was quoting Socrates. I continued the journal habit after college, keeping notes on students, and more particularly, wrestlers on the team I coached. During the season, I used the journal as a strategy book and weight loss record for my young charges. I also kept a record of my failing marriage, filling the pages with anger and frustration. The journal as therapy: it didn't solve anything, but it helped with the pain. When I retired from teaching and started working in the investigation business with Macintosh Thomas, ex-history teacher and truly amateur golfer, my notebooks became a moveable record of our cases. I also used them to keep track of our golf scores, notable games, and the enormous sums of money that Mack lost every time we played. I was also developing a compendium of memorable golf quotes, stories, and a list of my favorite golf movies: "Tin Cup," starring Kevin Costner and that great song by the Texas Tornadoes, "A Little Bit is Better Than Nada." Other titles Mack and I had agreed on included "Dead Solid Perfect," based on a book by Dan Jenkins; "Happy Gilmore," a nutty flick starring Adam Sandler, who plays a hockey player whose slap shot produces prodigious drives; "The Legend of Bagger Vance," a truly mystical film starring Will Smith and Matt Damon; "The Greatest Game Ever Played," a biopic about Francis Ouimet's win in the 1913 Open; and, of course, "Caddyshack," for out and out goofy fun.

Back to my latest entry:

Barney was dead, too. Barney was Stanley's constant companion. They ate together, went fishing together, slept together, drank beer together. They were found in Stanley's boat, each with a round bullet hole in his head. Barney was Stanley's dog, an oversized terrier mix of indeterminate age. They were both a couple of lovable mutts.

Stanley's boat was permanently docked at the marina near the Southport Golf Course. The boat was his summer residence, for he worked as dock master and guard from May to October. If one were to examine Stanley's life, he would find as many jobs as Barney had fleas. As a boy, Stanley had worked as a caddy on the golf course, among other teenage jobs, like mowing lawns and digging for clams. That was before the advent of the electric or gas-driven cart, when golf was played at a more leisurely pace. After a brief stint with the army in Italy, where he barely survived the hell of Anzio, Stanley returned to Southport, only to find that the club members did not enjoy looking at a hulking veteran with one ear and scars on his face. Stanley took employment as a groundskeeper, and supplemented his income by fishing, clamming, and working at the marina. Fired from the country club for drinking and generally lewd behavior, Stanley became a fisher of eels and golf balls at a treacherous hole modeled after the infamous third hole on the Mid-Ocean Course in Bermuda. The creek that meanders through the Southport Golf Course eventually empties into the bay. The tee is on one side of the little bay, and the green is on the other. Golfers have two options. They can play it safe, and hit the ball over the creek, then hit a second shot towards the green, triangulating the hole, as it were. The more adventuresome player could try to hit directly across the bay towards the green, and as it often happens on the hole on the Mid-Ocean, most of the drives wound up in the drink. Enter Stanley and Barney in a rowboat. Armed with an old clam rake, Stanley would scoop up the lost balls and either sell them back to the hapless golfers on the spot, or sell them to the club pro.

Stanley was also an unwashed, smelly Pied Piper to every kid in town. Growing up in Southport meant being repelled by and attracted to Stanley. Eventually curiosity and adventure would overcome fear and repulsion, and the lessons would begin. Like Caliban in Shakespeare's *Tempest*, Stanley knew "all the secrets of the island": the best places to tread for clams, where to fish for eels, how to catch a muskrat, how to clean a sea robin, where to get the biggest worms. All the good stuff every kid needs to know.

Once in awhile, Stanley and Barney would show up at a clambake or church social with a basket of eels. Dark, stringy hair under an old Yankee cap, a cloud of smoke billowing from a cigar of dubious origin, stained, dirty clothes caked with brine, fish blood, and other strange and mysterious fluids, muddy hip boots: Stanley could have stepped from a Wyeth painting. He had an uncanny nose for the most pretentious person at the gathering, usually a snooty member of the vestry or the Garden Club. Once he discerned his prey, he would sneak up behind the victim and slip a wriggling eel down the back of his shirt or her dress.

During the colder months, Stanley and Barney holed up in what everybody called "The Marsh House." Located on stilts in the wetlands, this humble abode probably got its start as a duck hunter's blind. When Stanley returned from the wars, he claimed squatter's rights, and proceeded to fix the place up. He put shingles on the roof and installed a small, potbellied wood stove. A door and a couple of windows were salvaged from a burned vacation cottage. Soon, the interior walls were decorated with the skulls of small wetland animals and the feathers of migratory birds. The furniture consisted of an old mattress, a chair, and a battered trunk. For lighting, there was a kerosene lantern and a couple of candles. On a shelf, there was a small collection of books: a Bible, *Moby Dick*, *Walden*, Peterson's *Field Guide to Birds*, *Siddhartha*. Stanley did not have a driver's license, but he had a library card.

Stanley was also very proud of his bottle garden. In the mud in front of the marsh house, there was a veritable jungle of bottles of all sizes, shapes, and colors, stuck neck-down in various depths and angles. By the light of a full moon, Stanley's strange and wonderful garden would take on a glistening life of its own, like some mystical, blue-green, faerie cityscape.

Who would kill this harmless old eccentric and his innocent dog?

Chapter 2

"Golf appeals to the idiot in us and the child. Just how childlike golf players become is proven by their frequent inability to count past five."—John Updike

"What are you writing, Sal?"

It was my partner, Mack Thomas. He leaned in the doorway, trying to catch his breath. Sweat slicked his scrawny neck. A bead of perspiration dropped from his hawk nose. Black going to gray hair drooped over his forehead. He looked like a cross between Abe Lincoln and Atticus Finch. Serious, yet boyish in a rumpled way, a perpetual twinkle in his eyes, as if he found life amusing.

"You're gonna have a heart attack one of these days, you keep pushing yourself. How many miles you go today?"

"Just a couple. I'm not crazy. You're just jealous."

With twenty extra pounds and a couple of bad knees, I had not jogged for a couple of years. Well, about ten years.

"I'm developing my mind." I waved at the computer and the books that lined the walls of Mack's garage, which also served as the office for our investigative agency. On the long table in front of me, there were a computer, a modem, telephone, fax machine, laser jet printer, and various other electronic toys. On the wall, amidst diplomas and certificates of appreciation, there were faded photos of Mack's first wife, Joan, who had died several years ago after a courageous bout with cancer. There were also shots of Mack and Joan and their kids, who were now grown up and starting families of their own. On the other side of the garage, there was an audio/ video set up, complete with cameras, editing machines, tape recorders, and a VCR. The far wall held part of Mack's extensive collection of books: the titles included such diverse works as Machiavelli's *The Prince*, Tom Paine's *Common Sense*, Adam Smith's *Wealth of Nations*, the complete Thoreau, Stowe's *Uncle Tom's Cabin*, Frazier's *The Golden Bough*, the writings of Confucius and Lao-Tze, the complete works of Dickens, Shakespeare, and Sir Arthur Conan Doyle, plus the complete works of Dick Francis, John D. Macdonald, Robert Parker, Phyllis Whitney, and Sue Grafton. Talk about eclectic tastes in reading matter, but you can tell a lot about a guy by the books he has on his shelf. There were also books on criminal and civil law and computer manuals to round out the collection.

Mack has learned very quickly that the life of a suburban sleuth is no where near the precincts of Sam Spade or Philip Marlowe. There is no colorful office on the seedy side of a large metropolis, no alluring and doting blonde secretary, no mysterious statues containing a fortune in gemstones. What we have is Mack's garage. The most exciting cases we have worked on have been a couple of cable TV theft-of-service and insurance fraud investigations, tracing wires from cable TV junction boxes and videotaping accident victims as they miraculously leap from wheelchairs to dance through the nearest shopping mall.

Mack said, "Mens sana in corpore sano, amigo."

"Yeah, yeah. Well, I prefer in *vino veritas*, as long as we're dragging out the high school Latin."

Looking at the computer screen, he said, "Still brooding about Stanley?"

"Yeah, I guess I am. You didn't know the old guy that well, but he and I went way back. Even went fishing together a couple of times."

Mack grunted. "Now there's a sport I could never get into. Sitting in the hot sun for hours, fighting boredom and mosquitoes, only to hook a slimy, smelly creature of the deep. I'd rather get my catch of the day from the fish store, thank you very much. Have the police come up with anything?"

We had a pretty good working relationship with the local cops. They tolerated us as amateurs, and we actually helped out the undersized force from time to time.

"You always were rather fastidious, but I won't hold that against you. No, the police seem to have lost interest in the case. Anyway, the thing that nags at me about Stanley is the lack of motive. Who would want to hurt the old guy? He never bothered anybody, except the occasional summer visitor with an eel down her frock. It's like you keep harping: motive, motive!"

Mack thought for a moment. "O.K. what are the chief motives in most crimes, Mr. Bones?"

"Fear...greed....love...revenge...I don't know. What else?"

"Well, that about covers it. Now, Stanley was so drunk most of the time, nobody was afraid of him. He was a threat to nobody but himself. Remember that time they found him face down in the snow? Wound up in the hospital for a couple of weeks. Greed? He never had any money, used the barter system most of the time, didn't even collect welfare or Social Security. Love? Revenge? I don't know. We'd have to dig deeper into his life. His mother must have loved him, but I can't imagine anybody else being able to get past the smell, as likeable as he was. Which brings us to the next question. I hate to bring up such crass considerations, but what's in this for us? If you'll forgive the pun, we've got bigger fish to fry."

"I know, I know. Let's just say I'm scratching an itch."

"Well, we'll have to do that when we've got some spare time. Meanwhile, we've got some paying customers who expect results."

By paying customers, my conscientious partner meant the Nagami Corporation, the new owners of the Treasure Oak Golf and Country Club.

When Mack and I retired from teaching a couple of years ago, we made a vow to play every golf course on Long Island, over a hundred courses. We were well on our way to reaching the goal when we came across the exclusive, members-only Treasure Oak

Course, located between Easthampton and Montauk Point. We were just about in position to wangle an invitation from a member when the course was sold to the Nagami Corporation, a giant electronics-media conglomerate with offices in New York, Los Angeles, and Tokyo. I had read in the *New York Times* about the Japanese efforts to buy the hallowed Pebble Beach course in California, so I was not surprised to see that their "golf-kichigai," loosely translated as "golf-craziness," had extended to the East Coast. According to *Sports Illustrated*, membership in a Tokyo golf club costs as much as two million dollars. Weekend greens fees run about $300, and golf balls, sold one at a time, cost about $8 each. Courses are so crowded it takes all day to play 18 holes, with the wait between shots usually longer than ten minutes. Playing golf, not necessarily well but enthusiastically, had become a corporate way of life for most Japanese, so it was not surprising that New York-based companies found the courses of nearby Long Island so inviting. What stunned the golfing establishment was the news that the Nagami Corporation had purchased the hallowed Treasure Oak Course, from the clubhouse to the last tee. It was as if the Disney enterprises had bought the Sistine Chapel. We were beginning to think we would never set foot on this fabulous course when we got a call from Brad Johnson, chief of the Southport Police Department.

"Sal? This is Brad Johnson."

"What's up, chief? Need help with the local crime wave?"

"Always a wise guy, that's what I like about you, Cascio. Anyway, I got something you guys might like to get involved in."

"No kidding, for real?"

"Yeah, yeah. Got a friend, Tom Yeager, Chief of Police out in Amagansett. Runs a small outfit, just him and two patrolman. It's the high tourist season and they're swamped out there."

"Didn't I read something about them putting a dummy in a patrol car to discourage speeders?"

"Yeah, and it worked, but the kids kept stealing the dummy. Listen, they got a complaint from the new owners of the golf course out there, the Japs."

"I don't think you're supposed to call them that, chief."

"Yeah, yeah, don't give me that politically correct bullshit. Just listen, will you? It seems there's been a lot of vandalism since they took over the course, but my friend doesn't have the manpower to look into it. He heard about you guys, couple of amateur detectives who liked to play golf, and called me to see if you were O.K."

I let the reference to "amateur" slide to see what else he had to say.

"Said he would bring you guys in as 'special consultants' if you were interested. Might satisfy the Japs if you went out there and looked around. Whatta ya say?"

"I'll have to talk to my partner, but give me your friend's number anyway. Sounds like an interesting situation."

When I told Mack, he said, "Let's call them. It's probably the only way we're going to set foot on the Treasure Oak, and who knows? In the course of our investigation, we may happen to have a golf club in our hand, and we may happen to drop a ball or two. We may happen to need a feel for the course if we're going to do the job right."

Chapter 3

Later that week, we were walking on the fabled course, accompanied by Chief Yaeger, Mr. Taro Yabe, representative from Nagami, and Ed Pearsall, the groundskeeper. The sun sparkled like gemstones on the dew-covered fairway. The air was crisp and clear, and it seemed as if every hole had a breath-taking view of the Atlantic Ocean. My fingers itched for the feel of a golf club as we walked down the fairway towards the first green. Working our way between two sand traps, we approach the edge of the first green, which was wide and deep and sloped away from the approach. We stood for a moment in stunned silence. The short, tender turf of the green had been torn apart by what seemed to be a giant stylus. The destruction had not been random, for it looked as if some sort of arcane symbol had been etched into the surface.

Mack said, "It looks like Japanese calligraphy. "

Mr. Yabe said, "Yes, there are two characters. They look like 'Nihongo kaerimasho,' roughly."

"What does that mean?"

"Loosely translated, it means "Japanese go home.""

The chief spoke up, "Sounds like we should get the County Bias Crimes Unit in here."

Mr. Yabe said, "No, no, not yet, please. We would prefer to proceed with a quiet, private investigation for the moment. We are satisfied with the recommendations for Mr. Cascio and Mr. Thomas. Let us see what they can find out."

The chief grumbled, "Well, if that's what you want. But if it gets any worse, or if you guys feel you're in over your head, give me a shout, O.K.? Meanwhile, before you repair the green, Ed, let me take a couple of pictures of that damage. Just for the record."

As we walked back to the clubhouse, Mr. Yabe informed us that the corporation had planned a big tournament next weekend. Would we be available to work as security?

Mack thought for a moment, then said, "I've got a better idea. How would you like to have the tournament videotaped? You know, introduce us as local photographers who will be filming highlights of the tournament to be shown at the awards dinner."

Mr. Yabe said, "Ah, I see. That way you would be able to move easily from one part of the course to another. "

"Yes, my associate here, Sal Cascio, is an excellent golf cart driver. He will drive, and I will operate the camcorder. "

What my partner failed to mention was that he needed me to drive because he was completely helpless when it came to operating any kind of vehicle. He even had trouble with his bicycle, which was his principal means of transportation since he lost his license many years ago. When Mack was still teaching, he rode his bicycle to school, and on the coldest mornings he could be seen wobbling into the school parking lot, an ungainly Ichabod Crane on a ten-speed bike.

On Saturday, Mack and I checked out a golf cart and cruised over to the first tee. The first foursome was already there, practicing golf swings, chatting, consulting the scorecard picture of the hole. The morning sun glistened on the fairway. There were no clouds in the deep blue sky. In the distance, sea birds wheeled and spun over the crashing surf. As the first player set the ball and lined up his driver, Mack started the camcorder. As soon as the first foursome hit their drives, we planned to zip over to the ninth hole, where another foursome would be starting their play. Then, as the tournament got under way, we would move from tee to fairway to green, getting a variety of shots. We had a list of players and the order of play, so we could make sure everyone appeared in the final version of the video.

Mack was setting up the camera on the ninth green when I heard a loud buzz overhead. It sounded like a couple of giant, angry hornets, and I looked up. Two small planes were flying towards us, so low that they just skimmed the treetops. I said to Mack, "Those guys are flying kind of low, aren't they?"

Mack swung the camera towards the approaching planes. I took a closer look, and it suddenly dawned on me that they weren't real planes, just very well-constructed models. The optical illusion was uncanny.

Mack said, "Hey, they look like the real thing. What are they? P-51's?"

"P-51 Mustangs? Didn't they use them in the war?"

The golfers stopped play and looked up, following the planes as they soared and cartwheeled over the course in a simulated aerial duel. Suddenly, one of the planes broke from the engagement and dove towards us. I had the weird feeling that if the plane were real, it would be opening fire and strafing us, bullets tearing into the green and golfers alike. I shook off the fantasy as the two planes roared overhead, waggling their wings in derision.

Mack said, "Whoever's operating those things knows their stuff, but they shouldn't be flying around here, and so low, either."

The Japanese golfers were chattering excitedly among themselves. Perhaps they thought the aerial show had been arranged for their entertainment; however, their initial amusement was beginning to sound like annoyance. There was a higher-pitched whine from above as the planes started another steep dive towards the green. This time, it didn't look as if they were going to be able to pull out of the dive. As the golfers scattered, I yelled to Mack, "Let's get out of the way, they're going to crash!"

As I jumped from the golf cart, I looked back. Mack held the camera steady on the planes, like a combat photographer. Suddenly, all hell broke loose. Just as the planes were about to hit the green, they exploded with a deafening roar. Bits of plastic and wood flew all over, and the green was covered with a cloud of acrid smoke.

I heard more buzzing, and looked up. A formation of six more planes was flying over the course, and as we watched in fascinated horror, each plane peeled off from the formation and began to attack other groups on the course. Golfers were running everywhere, looking for cover. Ironically, I was reminded of the Japanese attack on Pearl Harbor in the film, "From Here to Eternity." I wondered if the attackers had that in mind, too. Clearly, tournament play would have to be suspended for a while.

When the police arrived, we were able to give them a pretty good description of the planes, as well as Mack's videotape. Mr. Yabe was furious. The tournament was cancelled, and most of the players headed back to New York, chattering like irritated magpies. "Who would do this terrible thing?" he said.

Mack answered, "Clearly someone is making your life difficult, Mr. Yabe. Do you think this incident is connected to the damaged green you showed us?"

"I am sure it is. It is clearly a case of Japanese-bashing. I think it is a case for your bias crimes unit, chief."

The chief agreed with him, thanked us for our assistance, and basically told us to get lost. It was time for the big guns to investigate. Amateur hour was over.

As we left the clubhouse, Mack looked at the pristine fairways of the Treasure Oak Course and sighed, "We never got to hit a ball, but it was fun while it lasted."

Chapter 4

"Golf gives you an insight into human nature, your own as well as your opponent's."—Grantland Rice

The next day, I decided to go to the library and do some research. I Googled "model airplanes" and found a number of articles. A number of them were about groups on Long Island. This was not surprising, for Long Island is considered by many to be the cradle of modern aviation, Wright Brothers and Kitty Hawk notwithstanding. According to an article in *Newsday*, dated April 29, 1994, there were over 50 flying clubs on Long Island alone, with about 5,000 members. A lot of suspects to interview, I thought. One of the articles quoted a gentleman by the name of Tony Cassanello of Mastic Beach. Aha, I thought, a fine Sicilian name. Maybe he would be comfortable talking to another paisano.

Tony Cassanello was a gnomish, stooped mechanic recently retired from Grumman/Northrup Aviation. He had spent most of his working life crawling through narrow fuselages, wiring complicated flight systems. He had also been flying model airplanes for more than 45 years, and was eager to talk about his hobby: "It's a lot easier to fly a real plane visually than it is to fly a model from the ground, y'know. It's not a question of if you'll crash, but when. They ain't toys, and I got the scars to prove it." He showed me a gnarled hand, crisscrossed with scar tissue, calloused and disfigured. "These babies ain't cheap, either." He gestured to a Sopwith Camel, four to five feet in length, sitting on his workbench. "Guess how much that cost."

"I have no idea. $500?"

"Ya gotta be kidding. We're not talkin' rubber band engine here."

"So how much?"

"That's a fiberglass model, took about 200 hours to make, with a 25,000-RPM jet-type engine with ducted fan and exhaust pipe. When the electronics are installed, the remote controls, the bill comes to about $8,000."

"You've got yourself an expensive hobby. And I thought golf was bad."

"That ain't the half of it. I'm getting this baby ready for the annual Top Gun National Contest in Florida next month. So we're talking entrance fees and travel expenses."

"What's the contest like?"

"Man, it's fantastic. It's like watching the Blue Angels, with pattern flying and simulated bomb drops."

As he poured another glass of wine, I thought: "Who would load one of these expensive toys with explosives and intentionally blow it up over a golf course?" I voiced the question out loud, and added, "Do you know anybody who would be crazy enough to do such a thing? Anybody who's got a grudge against the Japs, maybe, like a vet?"

Tony thought for a moment, then answered, "You want to talk to Jimmy Mattas, he might know something."

"You got his number?"

"Better than that. I was going to go over to see him. You can tag along."

"I'll drive."

"Sure, whatever. But let me talk at first. Jimmy don't like nosy strangers."

The road to Jimmy's place was a winding, dirt track through the pine barrens northeast of Yaphank, a community with an interesting and varied past. Once it had been the summer resort for the German-American Nazi Bund. Then, ironically, it was the site of the staging camp for troops on their way to the trenches of World War I, immortalized by Irving Berlin in "Yip-Yip-Yaphank." There had been some talk of the town's reputation as a northern outpost of the Klan, and more recently, the John Birch Society. Nothing tangible, but it must have done wonders for real estate values. By the time we pulled up in front of Jimmy Mattus's place, it was hard to believe we were only 60 miles from Manhattan. Smoke curled from the stovepipe chimney of a rustic cabin that looked as if it belonged in the Ozarks. A thin old man, hunchbacked, leaning on a cane, stood on the porch. He had obviously heard us approach. I said to Tony, "How old is he, anyway."

"I think he's around 75-80, somewhere around there. He served in the Pacific during World War II."

I stopped the car, and Tony leaned out the window. "Hey, Jimmy, mind if we stop for a bit?"

Jimmy replied in a gravel voice, "Yer here, ain't ya? Might as well get out and sit for awhile."

I visualized a shotgun leaning against the wall just inside the front door, and what looked like a small barn in the woods behind the house.

Sitting on the porch, I felt like a kid listening to a couple of old timers swap lies and tall tales. I had been introduced as a "new friend," then ignored. Most of the talk was about model airplanes and the upcoming competition. It seems that Jimmy felt he was no longer able to travel, or could not afford the trip to Florida, and Tony was trying to talk him into it. Then Tony said, "Sal here has got an interesting story to tell you, Jimmy."

Responding to my cue, I related the story of the attack on the golf course. Aside from an occasional satisfied grunt and short laugh, Jimmy was silent. When I finished, he said, "Too bad they wasn't the real thing. The cops know anything?" There was a terrible gleam in his eyes.

"Not that I know of, not yet."

"Well, that's good. Maybe them Japs will go back where they belong."

Tony said, "Well, we gotta go, Jimmy. I'll call you next week about Florida."

Jimmy spat, and laughed bitterly, "Yeah, if I'm still alive and kicking."

As we drove away, I said, "Jimmy doesn't like the Japanese very much, that's pretty obvious. But what makes you think he could have done anything?"

Tony thought for a moment, then said, "Jimmy knows more about model airplanes than anybody I know. He was the best up to a couple of years ago, when his arthritis and old war injuries started to get to him. And he hates the Japs more than anybody."

"Well, I can understand that, considering his war injuries. But after all these years, and Hiroshima and all that?"

"You know what got to him more than anything else?"

"What?"

"Hearing that the Japanese-Americans held in detention camps were going to get $20,000 apiece for their so-called pain and suffering."

"Yeah, I heard about that. But don't you think they deserved some compensation? After all, they were American citizens, and some of their relatives were fighting in Italy, distinguishing themselves in battle."

"Yeah, yeah. Well, Jimmy was captured, and survived the Bataan Death March. He saw guys decapitated, burned alive, starved to death. He almost died, himself. He said a lot of people don't realize how many people the Japanese killed in concentration camps. And for this, the U.S. government paid him about $2.00 a day. So how do you think he feels when he sees Japanese over here, all over our golf courses, buying up our real estate? Yeah, I'd say he's got a reason to be bitter."

Chapter 5

"Golf is a game that is played on a five-inch course: the distance between your ears."—Bobby Jones

A week later, I watched as Mack lost a second ball to the infamous bay that separated the third fairway of the Southport Golf Course.

"Should've played it safe," I said, "and hit over the creek."

"Yeah, yeah. I know," Mack answered, as he reached into his bag for another ball.

"Too bad old Stanley isn't around to fish out your lost balls."

"Yeah, this hole just isn't the same. I kind of miss the old coot, sitting with his dog in the rowboat out there in the bay, just waiting for guys like us to come along and make fools of ourselves."

"Speak for yourself, my man. I don't usually wind up in the drink. Don't you know you're supposed to use a seven wood to hit over that stretch of water? You going to hit again, or take a stroke and join me on the other side?"

Mack looked at the ball in his hand, then said, as if thinking out loud, "Nothing has come up about his murder. The police don't seem to care…"

"Well, get real. They don't usually get too worked up about drifters, low-profile cases. Just another bum out of the way, you know."

"Wait a minute, Stanley wasn't just another homeless bum. He was a local institution, almost. He had a history with a lot of people around here."

"I know that, and you know it. But you get my point—he isn't important enough to make a fuss about it. I'm sure he's in some detective's notebook, but not as a high priority item."

"So maybe we should help out a little. As a public service. "

"Oh-oh, I know that routine. The last time we helped out a little, it landed you in the hospital—twice."

"Well, if was a little faster on my feet..."

"Mack, the last time you were fast on your feet, you were running away from an elementary school bully."

"Sure, sure. I don't see you dancing the night away on your mangled kneecaps, either. But seriously, I think we could spend a little time around the marina, ask some questions, do a little schmoozing, see what turns up."

"Sounds good to me."

Mack lined up his putt, stroked, and watched his ball shoot past the cup. It sat precariously on the edge of the green for a moment, then dropped ignominiously into the sand trap on the far side.

As he climbed out of the trap, he said, "What's happening with your search for the mad bombers of Nagami?"

"Not much. I have one guy that might make a good suspect, guy by the name of Jimmy Mattus. Angry old vet who lives up in the woods near Yaphank. "

"Did you say anything to the police?"

"Nah, I didn't have anything concrete. Besides, since that disability exposé, I'm philosophically opposed to doing the cops' work for them."

"I don't blame you. It's not as if you have all sorts of extra time these days. "

I thought about Mack's last remark. In the last month, my life had become incredibly complicated. When I retired from teaching, I looked forward to a bachelor's dream: an unending string of sunny days of golf, going to the track, fishing; long, smoke-filled nights of gambling and other forms of debauchery; reading my way through the public library; going to every home Knicks game. Nirvana. Then I got hooked into Mack's retirement dream, the private investigation business.

Here's how I got involved in Mack's dream. There's an old saying,

"Those who can't do, teach." Nobody involved in teaching for more than five years takes this canard seriously. We had taught history, civics, economics, social awareness, and psychology for thirty years in a tough school, learning to deal with students and parents ranging from the gifted to the psychotic, thinking up all kinds of head games to compete with the distractions of raging hormones, insidious drugs, and non-stop MTV, making the proverbial thousand decisions a day, finding out why Dick can't read at age 17 and how Jane got pregnant at age 14, introducing functional illiterates to Dosteovsky, Dickens, and Dreiser. Over the years, we had become pretty good students of human nature, and that, my friend, qualified us to be private investigators.

Recently, my wayward former wife came back to town. We have started to see each other, tentative get-togethers over a cup of coffee and a shared piece of lemon meringue pie, thinking about re- building a new life together, not an easy feat for a stubborn paisano, but I'm trying, and I think Carol appreciates that. The thing that has made our lives incredibly complicated is that at the age of 67 and 62 respectively, we have become the parents of a set of rambunctious twins.

Chapter 6

"They say golf is like life, but don't believe them. Golf is more complicated than that." —Gardner Dickinson

Here's how it happened. When we were married, Carol and I had two children, a boy and a girl, Sal and Teresa. Sal became a surgeon in a hospital in Pittsburgh, lives with a lovely wife and kids in the suburbs. Life was not so good for Teresa, our baby. She was a beautiful little girl, fatherly prejudice notwithstanding. Long, black hair, sparkling eyes, a laugh like a crystal bell, the kid was a charmer. Dance class, gymnastics, piano lessons, cheer leading: it was as if she lived to please everybody around her. Right after high school graduation, she announced that she was going to marry Nick, a ne'er do well with no prospects. The kind of guy every father wants his daughter to stay away from. Black, greasy hair, a number of run-ins with the local constabulary, a reputation as a doper and brawler. We were not overly excited. While her grades were not the best, I thought she would be able to find herself academically at the local community college, then maybe transfer to a four-year school. Carol was not too happy about Nick's reputation, but our marriage was beginning to slide towards disaster, and to tell the truth, we were so preoccupied with our own problems, we just didn't pay enough attention to what was going on with Teresa, and caved into her plans for marriage, if you call a quick flight to Las Vegas that.

About a year ago, Teresa called in a panic. Nicky had left her. No, she didn't know where he had gone. She was sick. Nothing to worry about. Could Mack and I watch the twins when she went into the hospital for some tests?

Teresa never came out of the hospital. It turned out that dear old Nicky was an intravenous drug user, HIV positive, and had infected his wife and the mother of his children with AIDS. Teresa, never very strong, died after the first onslaught of pneumonia. For a while, I truly believe I would have been able to commit murder. I still do, at times.

So the grandparents have become parents, once again, and Carol and I have a new complication to our relationship.

Chapter 7

"I know I am getting better at golf because I'm hitting fewer spectators." —Gerald Ford

Mack's domestic situation has changed, too. A couple of years ago, he lost his wife to cancer. It was a long, lingering, painful death, made a little easier by the caring presence of Maria Sanchez, a nurse who had immigrated to the United States from the bloody strife of El Salvador.

According to Mack, Maria was born in a small fishing village on Lake Ilopango, near the capital of El Salvador. She married young, at the age of 17, and her husband Carlos had a good job as a mechanic at a local garage. They had two children, Juan and Carmelita. In 1980, the peaceful countryside became a landscape of horror. Headless bodies began to turn up in vacant lots and public restrooms. Thugs prowled the streets in armored Cherokees, firing indiscriminately into crowds in the marketplace. Vultures haunted the garbage-filled ravines, feeding on the dead. Such unfortunates were called "Los desaparacidos y los muertos," the disappeared and the dead. One evening Maria had come home from her job at La Clinica to find her children in tears. Five men had pushed their way into the garage, dragged Carlos out from under a car, thrown him into the back of a Cherokee, and roared off in a cloud of dust. As the tension-filled days passed, Maria learned that Las Orejas, "the ears," informers, had named her husband to a death list. Maria suspected the owner of the other garage in town, but couldn't prove anything. When she head about the death list, Maria decided to take the children and to into hiding with relatives in another province. Four or five months passed, with no word from Carlos. The children cried at night, and they viewed any strange car in the village with fear. Soon Maria could wait no longer. She sold their belongings and made a contract with a man in the village who claimed to be a coyote, a guide who would take them north. Their first stop was a refugee camp in Guatamala, a terrible place filled with diarrhea and dehydration. After many days on a wheezing bus, they arrived at a small village near the border between Mexico and the United States.

On the night of their border crossing, dark rain clouds slid across the sky, obscuring the moon. Their guide took them as far as the border, then gave one of the men in the group a cheap compass, a flashlight, and a few canteens of water. "Keep walking north," he said, "until you come to a blacktop highway. Walk in either direction until you come to a town, then go to the nearest church. They will take care of you. Watch out for La Migra."

Confused and frightened, Maria and her children followed the men as they trudged northward. Little did they know that they had ahead of them a fifty-mile trek through one of the worst deserts in the Southwest. Half of the party would die, including Maria's daughter, Carmelita. As Juan and Maria stumbled on to the blacktop highway, a pickup truck driven by a Navaho farmer appeared. The driver took them into his home, and he and his wife nursed the survivors back to health, as is the Navaho custom. Yes, Maria had known the face of death.

After his wife's death, Mack and I had been instrumental in helping her son Juan, who for a short time had been a suspect in the murder case of our former boss. Since then, Mack and Maria had grown close, and Mack had been giving advice and emotional support to the angry young Juan, slowing bringing him into the mainstream of American life. I think Mack and Maria were still in the healing stage, for they were still going through a very polite and restrained courtship.

There was something almost stylized and graceful about it, and at times I felt like an old-fashioned duenna, following the couple around the village square on a warm summer evening, making sure they did not kiss. Metaphorically speaking, that is.

Juan was another story. Losing his father at a young age, crossing the desert with his mother and watching his sister die, frustrated by language and social barriers in school, dropping out, falsely accused by the police: the kid had more than his share of problems growing up. It was a wonder he wasn't a basket case. If it weren't for the strength and fortitude of his mother, and eventually the support and concern from Mack, the kid would probably have gone down the tubes. I am proud to say I had a small part in his rehabilitation. I speak a little Spanish (with an Italian accent), and was able to help Juan get his GED high school equivalency certificate. Mack tutored him also, and together we were able to get him into the local community college.

All of these efforts pointed towards a new life for Mack. Marriage with Maria was a distinct possibility, and he was committed to putting another young man through college.

Our fledgling private investigation business was about to become more than an avocation, for suddenly, there were a few mouths to feed.

Chapter 8

"In golf, you keep your head down and follow through. In the vice presidency, you keep your head up and follow through. It's a big difference." —Dan Quayle

It was a Saturday morning in April. Carol and Maria had taken the twins to the park for an outing, so Mack and I had a chance to catch up on some paperwork. Time had suddenly become a precious commodity, for Carol was going back to school to get a real estate agent's license, and Maria was working 30 to 40 hours a week at a local hospice. Lately, Mack's garage-office has been resembling a day-care center, but today, we had work to do. Still curious about the attack on the Japanese-owned golf course, I was looking at the directory of model airplane retail outlets in the New York area. Mack was on the telephone, talking to the owner of the marina where Stanley was found dead. It was a pro bono morning, for neither of these endeavors would result in any investigative fees. There were some insurance reports and bills to be made out, however, so we would have diaper and formula money for the next month.

Mack hung up the phone and said, "You know, Steve over at the marina said that Stanley kept bugging him about hearing strange noises late at night. Kept talking about swamp ghosts, pirates, and buried treasure, that kind of thing. At the time, Steve chalked it up to the delusional babble of an old rummy."

"Delusional babble? Did Steve say that?"

"No, but words to that effect. You know what I mean. Stanley was prone to the occasional tall tale. In fact, that was part of his rough charm."

"Yeah, as long as you weren't downwind of him."

"I wonder if Stanley saw or heard something he wasn't supposed to witness?"

At that point, there was a knock on the door. It was Juan, Maria's son.

"Juan! Qué tal? What's happening, kid?"

"Good morning, Mack, Señor Sal. How are you?"

Mack picked up some books, making space on a bench. "Come on in, Juan. What's up? How's school going? Still having some problems with that lit class?"

Mack had been tutoring Juan, leading him through the intrigues of *King Lear.* It was hard enough for Juan, for whom English was a recently acquired language. What made things more difficult was having to read the play in Elizabethan English, in class, which I am sure is something Shakespeare himself did not intend.

"Shakespeare himself intended the plays to be seen, not stumbled through and analyzed to death," he said.

"You mean murdered by dissection."

"O.K. Wordsworth. You get the idea. Anyway, thank god for guys like Kenneth Branagh. His films have brought the Bard back to life, at least for the younger generations."

He said to Juan: "Did you see that Olivier video from the library?"

Juan responded, "Yes, I saw it. It was very good, and I think I am beginning to understand the play. He was a foolish old man, to test his daughters' love that way."

I said, "Well, love makes us do foolish things."

Mack chimed in, "Yes, Señor Cascio is an expert in that field."

Before I could punch Mack, Juan said, somewhat urgently, "I must ask you a question, Mack."

"What's the problem, son?"

"Well, I have been asked to join this club at the college."

"What's wrong with that? You should be pleased. What club?"

"It's called the 'Ecology Club,' and they take field trips to the wetlands and clean up the beaches. It sounded like a nice thing."

"Sounds like it to me. So what's wrong?"

"I went to the first meeting, thinking I would see some girls, and you know, what Señor Cascio calls 'tree-huggers,' but most of the members are football players. They spent most of the time talking about clamming and boats and something called 'product.' I felt they were talking in some kind of code, but my English, as you know, is not perfect yet. I still have trouble with, what do you call it, Mack?"

"Idiomatic expressions?"

"Yes, that is it. I could not understand why I had been invited to join this club. I do not play football. I know nothing about clamming or boats. I know about plants and growing things from working on the golf course, but they did not want to hear about my experiences there."

Mack thought for a minute. "I don't know, Juan. What special skill do you have that the average junior college jock doesn't?"

Juan said, "I don't know. I was the only Spanish-speaking person at the meeting, maybe that is it."

I said, "Now what would the Ecology Club want with a person who speaks Spanish and English? Maybe they're going to Puerto Rico on the winter break."

Mack said, thoughtfully, "No, I think there's more to it than that. Juan, why don't you go ahead and join that club, and tell us if they do anything that sounds strange."

Chapter 9

"The only time my prayers are never answered is on the golf course." —Billy Graham

As the poet said, "April is the cruelest month," and the Iron Age is returning to Long Island, Golf Irons, that is. In the early morning mist, the tender, young grass of spring quivers as the rumble of gas-driven golf carts is heard in the distance. Like primitive savages, the hookers, the slicers, the choppers begin their annual quest for the Holy Grail, praying that maybe this year, the hope springs eternal, maybe this year they will break par.

Mack scoffed at my dream as he teed up on the first hole of the Indian Head Golf Course, a municipal course owned and operated by the county. The wait for a starting time had been, in darkness, with dozens of other early birds as the early morning sun gradually warmed our bones. There is something atavistic, primitive about rising before dawn, taking up weapons, girding for combat with a bagel and a cup of coffee, standing on the field of battle with the other combatants, watching the steamy fog rise from the fairways.

If you look at Long Island on a map, from east to west it looks like a giant fish, with two fins sticking out in the back. Looking at the island from west to east, the fins become the jaws of a monster. Depending on whether your view of things is benign or malignant, the Indian Head Golf Course is on an island held between the fins, or about to be consumed by the jaws. At any rate, it has a lovely view of Peconic Bay, home of the world's best scallops and succulent clams.

As we walked down the first fairway, I looked out over the bay, and saw the clam boats drifting through the receding mist. The long, wide, shallow-draft boats would pause every fifty yards or so, and deposit a muscular young man in a wet suit, equipped with an inner tube, a short-handled clam rake, and a peach basket.

Mack said, "I wonder if any of those guys are Leroy's Boys?"

"Leroy's Boys" were high school football players recruited by Leroy Kemp, the coach at the school where Mack and I worked before retirement. Kemp owned a couple of clam boats. In the spring and summer, he offered the players employment—with clams going for $50 a basket, a kid could make $400-500 a week, even after paying the coach his fee for transportation, equipment, food and drink—as well as fresh air and exercise. Clamming is hard work. Pulling a rake all day and pushing the legs against the tide, according to Kemp, was better than running and pumping iron. Besides, pumping iron didn't make money. So it was a good deal for everyone involved. There were some who applauded Kemp for taking poorer kids off the streets during the long, hot summers and giving them meaningful employment. Kemp's critics saw him as a modern-day Fagin who profited from his involvement with youth. Regardless of either camp, Kemp's teams usually wound up in the play-offs, and by the time they were seniors, most of the clammers were driving to school in brand new 4X4's, Cherokees, Jeeps, Blazers, Pathfinders, and other expensive toys. Each vehicle gleamed with chrome accessories, was wired for wall-to-wall sound, and sported tires the size of small elephants.

Unfortunately, the care and feeding of these road beasts kept most of the team away from the library, and with a few rare exceptions, the team wound up at the local community college after graduation. The operative euphemism was "for a little academic polishing." In reality, most of the players wound up in the remedial classes offered by the college, and occasionally, in the classes that were designed to get them ready for the remedial work itself. As a state-operated, open enrollment school, the community college was obligated to accept any high school graduate, whether he could read or not. The kids sported that teenage status symbol, the beeper, and lately, had been seen carrying cell phones.

Youngsters who went on to four-year colleges more often than not were served up as fresh meat for the varsity to feast on during practice. After a couple of years, the new NCAA academic standards caught up with them, and they were declared ineligible. After flunking out, they returned home to careers in lawn maintenance, automotive repair, and trash recycling. In a way, the community college candidates had a better opportunity, for at least they got a second chance at the academic side of things. Besides, they got to commute in those fancy trucks of theirs.

Chapter 10

"Golf is the cruelest game, because eventually it will drag you out in front of the whole school, take your lunch money, and slap you around." —Rick Reilly

The next day, after taking more money out of my golfing partner's wallet, I got a call from Chief Yaeger. After the opening pleasantries, he said, "You and Mack busy?" I know he knew we were not, but said, "Well, we have a couple of things we're working on."

He said, "The Invasion of the Summer People is upon us, and my staff is quickly becoming overwhelmed." He was right. During the summer months on Long Island, the traffic virtually multiplies like a virulent disease, spreading from the highways to the byways with alarming speed, choking any kind of vehicular movement to the point of sudden death.

His small department had their hands full dealing with traffic and the numerous complaints of tourists of every variety.

He said, "How would you and Mack feel about becoming temporary deputies? Helping us out with that golf course problem?"

I said, "Let me check with my partner. Knowing him, I'm sure he would be glad to lend a hand, especially if we can get back on the Treasure Oak Golf Course."

When I broached the subject with Mack the next day, he said, "You know, I've been thinking about the day the planes attacked. I think we need to get a different perspective on the situation, a bird's eye's view, as it were."

"What do you mean?" I said.

"You know Jim Rooney, the guy who runs Eagle Eye Aerial Photography?"

I knew Jim. He was an old pro, a photographer with an single engine airplane who specialized in aerial shots of just about anything that was of interest to the local newspapers: brush fires, traffic accidents, things like that. Mack continued, "I want to go up with him, take a look at the course from the perspective of a would-be dive bomber."

The next day, we found ourselves crammed into the cabin of a Cessna 250, flying over the island. Mack shouted over the engine noise, "Look at the barrier beach. It looks as if the last big Nor'easter has wiped out most of the sand dunes across from the golf course."

I looked in that direction. I said, "With one more storm, there could be an inlet across from the course."

Mack said, "Yes, the ocean would wash over the barrier beach, and an inlet could be formed."

As we flew towards the course, I could see clam diggers dotting the surface of the bay, forming a loose circle around the boat belonging to the manager of the Kemp operation.

"Look down there," Mack shouted, "There's the creek where Stanley did most of his golf ball business."

From our height and perspective, it seemed that many of these elements were related in some way: the golf course, the suspicious clam enterprise, Stanley's old haunts. I thought: "Odd that these things that bother us are so close, geographically." I planned to discuss this further with Mack once we landed.

Rooney shouted at us over the prop noise, "You guys are back on that Treasure Oak case?"

"Yeah, we're back on it, been deputized as a matter of fact."

Rooney said, "Ever hear anything about the legend of the Treasure Oak? That a real pirate's treasure is buried somewhere near or on the course?"

Mack Said, "I heard something about that. Probably dug up a long time ago, though."

When we landed, Mack had a funny look on his face. I knew that look well. He pursed his lips, wrinkled his forehead, narrowed his eyes, as if something was really bugging him, but he didn't quite know what it was.

"I'll see you later," he said, "I'm going to the library to do some research."

Chapter 11

"Golf is a good walk spoiled."—Mark Twain

This is what Mack found out: Long Island, formerly called Nassau Island in Colonial times, was a popular haunt of real pirates, especially the East End. Richard Coote, the Colonial governor of New York, complained about East End piracy in a letter written in 1699, saying that the islanders were "so lawless and desperate a people that I can get no honest man to venture among them and collect their excise." William Kidd, known later as Captain Kidd, was appointed by Coote to the position of pirate-hunter on the high seas, a position he apparently took to with great fervor. Kidd never considered himself a pirate, but called himself a privateer, a distinction lost on the King and his governor after Kidd and his 150-man crew seized the *Quedah Merchant* in the spring of 1698. After learning he had been branded as a pirate by his former sponsors, Kidd decided to regain his reputation in a court of law, using the Quedah and other seized treasure as bargaining chips. On the way to Boston, he stopped at Gardiner's Island, reportedly buried his treasure at Cherry Harbor. He told the island's owner, Jonathan Gardiner, "If I call for it and it is gone, I will take your head, or your son's." The threat proved to be idle, for Kidd was found guilty and hanged in London. The island was overrun by a band of pirates, and Kidd's treasure disappeared.

The Long Island Studies Institute at Hofstra University put together a special collection in 2006 called "Pirates of Long Island: the Curse of the Twin Forks." There was Joseph Bradish, considered more fierce than Kidd, who seized cargo worth about $400,000. Then there was the notorious "Handy" Jones, who worked the Great South Bay in the early 1780's. Handy would hide in the shallow-draft sloops of the bay men overnight, and when they set sail the next day, he would jump out of hiding and throw them overboard. If they tried to climb back aboard, he would cut off their hands with the hatchet he always carried. Finally, there was Charlie Gibbs, a real fiend who is believed to have killed 400 people. After failing in the liquor business in Boston, Gibbs went pirating. He recalled, "When I robbed my first ship, my conscience made a hell in my bosom, but after I sailed the black flag for a number of years, I could rob a vessel and murder every passenger on it and sleep soundly." He would bury his treasure on Barren Island, in the southern end of Jamaica Bay. After he was caught and sentenced to hang, he uttered, or was reported to have uttered, probably the most famous line in pirate history: "No mercy did we ever show because dead men tell no tales."

Mack found stories about modern-day pirates, accounts of hijacking and murder aboard million dollar pleasure craft in the Caribbean, especially along the coasts of Venezuela and Colombia. As for North American pirates, he thought, they had morphed into venture capitalists, hedge fund managers, and corporate raiders. "The more things change, the more they remain the same," he said to himself.

Chapter 12

"Golf is an ineffectual attempt to put an elusive ball into an obscure hole with implements ill-adapted to the purpose."
—*Woodrow Wilson*

A week later we found ourselves on the Treasure Oak Golf Course once again. We had been given a golf cart, and armed with a camcorder and a couple of golf clubs, we started patrolling the course. The camcorder was to record any salient evidence; the golf clubs were for self-protection, just in case we happened to come across a lost ball in the rough that needed to be sent on its way. It was a weekday, and there were few tournaments scheduled lately, so we pretty much had the course to ourselves. The temperature was in the eighties, the air balmy, with a soft breeze wafting in from the bay.

Mack said, "On a day like today, it's hard to think that there is evil in the world."

I answered, "All you have to do is pick up the newspaper, look at the casualty list from Iraq, read about the motor vehicle accidents on the Expressway, check out the Mets' losing streak, the latest exploits of Paris Hilton. Yes, all is not right with the world."

Mack frowned, then said, "You know, it isn't. Juan came home from school the other day with a black eye, a real shiner. And some cuts and bruises. He looked like he really got into it with someone."

"Did he say who it was?" I asked.

"No, he went right into the bathroom and took a shower. Then he went into his room, got dressed, and went out again before I had a chance to talk to him."

"Was Maria there?"

"No, she was working. If she had been home and seen him, I don't think she would have let him out of the house without an explanation."

"Have you seen him since then?"

"No, everybody seems to be so busy these days, we can't even sit down to dinner together. Juan's taking night classes, and we work during the day. Maybe we'll catch up with him this weekend."

Just then we spotted a lone golfer walking down an adjacent fairway, pulling a bag of clubs. He looked like a cross between Rip Van Winkle and the Ancient Mariner, with shabby army fatigues and a long, flowing white beard.

Mack said, "Who's that guy? I haven't seen him before."

"He certainly doesn't look like a member," I said. "Let's check him out."

By the time we crossed over onto the other fairway, the old golfer had disappeared.

During that week, we saw the old guy a few more times, but usually from a distance. Every time we tried to catch up with him, he had disappeared. Mack said, "He must be jumping from hole to hole, not following the course the way it's laid out."

I said, "Yeah, and every time he sees us coming, he probably ducks into the woods. Definitely a suspicious character."

Mack laughed, "Or probably an old guy who lives nearby, who just sneaks on to play a few holes when it isn't busy."

"I don't know. This guy is beginning to bug me. Go back to the club house. I'm going to hide in the bushes and see if I can flush this bird."

About an hour after Mack had left, I began to think that lying in hiding was not such a good idea. The bugs were beginning to bite, and I was hot and thirsty. I was just about to give up, when sure enough, I heard a kind of tuneless whistling, and heading towards me was the old geezer, chasing his ball down the fairway. I jumped out onto the fairway and grabbed his ball.

"Hey, watcha doin' with my ball? Yer crazy, or sump'n?" He came rushing up to me, waving a seven iron in a threatening fashion.

"Whoa, partner. Put the club back in your bag, and I'll return your ball. I just wanted to talk to you for a minute."

When I placed his ball a bit closer to the green, he seemed to calm down a bit. I presented my deputy's documents and said, "Are you a member, sir?"

He grumbled, "No, not really. I used to belong, many years ago, before the new management took over. It don't seem too busy these days, so I thought I'd come out and hit a couple of balls."

"What's your name, fella?"

"What are you gonna do, write me a ticket? Arrest me?"

"No, I just plan to escort you off the course, sir. Let me give you a ride to the entrance."

"Well, if I gotta go…"

He didn't say anything else as we loaded his bag on the back of my golf cart and headed off the course. He still hadn't identified himself, so I said, "I see you're wearing fatigues. Are you a vet?"

"Yeah, I was in 'Nam, but nobody cares."

"Well, some do. I was in Korea myself."

He was quiet for a moment, then said, "I hear that was no picnic."

I told him about my near-death experience. I was in a communications unit, and my job was to climb poles and keep the wires repaired. One day I was up on a pole, trying to figure out a connection, when some North Koreans came along. They started shooting at me, but they were kids, not very good shots. One hit me in the leg, though, and I yelled in pain. Then I had a bright idea. I slumped over, hanging in my harness. They hung around for a while, then decided I was dead or about to die, and walked off. That little bit of play acting got me a month of R&R in Tokyo.

He was quiet for awhile, then said, "I used to live around here, but after 'Nam, I sort of wandered around the country, kind of looking for what I was fighting for, I guess."

"What brings you back to these parts?"

"I had a brother still living here. That is, he used to live here, but he was killed."

"Don't tell me…was his name Stanley?"

Chapter 13

"Years ago we discovered the exact point, the dead center of middle age. It occurs when you are too young to take up golf and too old to rush up to the net." —Franklin Pierce Adams

When we got to the clubhouse, I parked the cart and said to my passenger, whose name turned out to be Henry, "How about a couple of old vets sitting down over a beer or cup of coffee?"

"I wouldn't mind, but not here. This place is too rich for my blood."

It occurred to me that the course was not too rich for him, but kept that thought to myself. "How about a cup of coffee, then? There's a good place down the road called the Modern Snack Bar. They have great pie."

A few minutes later, Henry and I were sitting down over coffee and the best rhubarb pie on Long Island. I told him I had known Stanley for many years, but never heard of a brother.

He said, "He was the proverbial black sheep of the family. Our parents tried to help him, but he was always different, strange. He would go off by himself for days, even as a teenager. Nobody knew where he went. I tried to follow him once, but lost him in the wetlands. After our parents were killed in an automobile accident, he disappeared for good. It was around then that I enlisted in the army before getting drafted."

"How come you came back now?" I asked.

"I was living in Key West, pretty much on the beach. Doing some fishing, odd jobs. I met some folks from around here on a fishing boat. I asked them if they knew Stanley, and they said they did. I didn't tell them I was his brother. Anyway, they told me about him getting killed, so I had to come back to find out more about it."

"Have you learned anything?" I asked.

"No. At first the cops thought I was a homeless person, and wanted to run me out of town. Then I showed them my vet's credentials. That settled them down, but they couldn't tell me anything about Stanley, said they hadn't gotten the forensics report yet. Next thing I did, I looked up the family lawyer, Jack Hart, and he told me I was named in Stanley's will."

"Stanley had a will? What for?" I asked. "I didn't think he owned anything, except maybe that broken-down old boat."

Henry snorted. "That's what everybody believed, they thought he was a broken-down old bum, but guess what? He not only owned that boat, but also the piece of land where the Marsh House was built. Did you know that he also had a bank account with about $10,000 in it?"

I had heard that an artist from New York, who was particularly taken with the bottle garden, had wanted to buy the Marsh House, use it for a studio, something like that. But $10,000? That's a lot of retrieved golf balls.

I said, "Where did Stanley get $10,000? It couldn't have been for the Marsh House. That was built on the wetlands. I'm not sure he had legal claim to the land."

Henry said, "I don't know. The banker just said he came in several months ago, and made a deposit of $10,000. Said he planned to make another deposit soon. Then he was killed."

Chapter 14

"Golf may be played on Sunday, no being a game within the view of the law, but being a form of moral effort."
—Stephen Leacock

The next day, I told Mack what I had learned from Henry.

He said, "So Stanley had a brother, did he? And $10,000 in the bank?"

"Yeah, with more to come."

"That certainly sounds suspicious to me. Stanley never saw that much money in his life. Maybe we should talk to the police about this."

I said, "Henry said he didn't get anywhere with them, but they didn't seem to give him the time of day."

Mack said, "There's something rotten in the state of Denmark, my friend."

At this point, the telephone rang. It was Carol, calling from the hospital. No, there was nothing wrong with the twins, nor her. It was Juan. He had been brought to the hospital by the local ambulance company. He was unconscious, with a gash in his head. Maria was with him, barely hanging on the edge of hysteria.

Mack said, "We'll be right there, Carol. Tell Maria we're coming."

We jumped into my car and broke a number of traffic laws getting to the hospital. We were stopped once, but after the patrolman realized who we were, that I was the guy who had coached his son to a championship, he escorted us, siren blaring, to the front door of the hospital. Small towns can be like that, you know.

Carol met us at the door, saying, "He's still unconscious. Maria's up there with him. I have to go, a neighbor's watching the kids. Call me, Sal, when you find out anything." A quick kiss on the cheek and she was off like a whirlwind.

When we got to Juan's room, a doctor was outside, talking to Maria. "He will be O.K." he said. "Head wounds bleed a lot, but there was no major damage. Just an ugly gash that we stitched up. He may be a little concussed, but there's no skull fracture."

Maria, even though she had medical training, looked as if she was about to faint. Mack stepped up to her and put his arm around her shoulders. We spend the rest of that night sitting with Maria in the hospital, keeping a vigil over a sleeping young man.

Chapter 15

"Golf is not, on the whole, a game for realists. By its exactitudes of measurement it invites the attention of perfectionists." — *Heywood Hale Broun*

Juan regained consciousness the next day, much to our relief. He was still a bit groggy, but in bits and pieces was able to tell us what had happened. The "Ecology Club" had planned an outing to Robins Island, a bird sanctuary out in the middle of Great South Bay. The clamming was supposed to be good there, and a bunch of club members who were also clam diggers were going to be there too. The only odd thing about the expedition was that it was going to take place late in the day.

Juan said, "It was my understanding that the best time to see birds is early in the morning. Also, clam diggers usually went out early too, depending on the tides. But they said this was going to be special."

Juan decided to go anyway, out of curiosity, but was surprised when Ted Bukowski, one of the older members, came up to him and told him he was not going on this trip.

"I couldn't figure out why they didn't want me to go. Maybe it was because I was a new member."

After everyone set out for the island, Juan's curiosity got the better of him. He launched his kayak, a birthday present from Mack, and set out across the bay. He arrived at the island just as the sun was setting, and hid out of sight in some reeds along the shore.

As darkness began to settle, Juan saw that the clam diggers had arranged themselves in a wide circle, and each one was holding a flashlight. Then Juan heard the sound of an airplane. He said, "It sounded like a private aircraft, a single engine plane, like the one Mack's friend uses to take photographs from the air."

As the plane flew overhead, dozens of packages about the size of beach balls began to splash into the circle formed by the clam diggers. The diggers pulled the packages from the water and put them in their baskets, and began moving towards a boat that had just pulled up.

Juan said, "I could not see who was operating the boat, it was too dark by then." When the clam diggerss reached the boat, they began dumping their packages, tubes, and baskets into the well and climbed aboard.

At that moment, Juan decided to head back for the mainland. As he started to paddle away from his hiding spot, he heard a shout from the boat. He paddled faster, hoping to get out of sight. Soon he was located by a powerful spot light from the boat that had picked up speed and was bearing down on him. The last thing he knew was the crash.

Fortunately, Juan's attackers didn't know that he was a survivor, had seen and lived through worse than they could ever think to deal out to him. In spite of his injuries, the shock of the water revived him enough so he could swim to a sailboat moored off shore. He climbed aboard, and passed out.

The next morning, the sailboat owner found an unconscious, bloodied young man lying in the cockpit, and called the police on his cell phone.

Chapter 16

"I do much of my creative thinking while golfing."
—Harper Lee

A few days later, while Juan was still convalescing in the hospital, Mack and I were sitting in the office. He was cleaning his clubs, something he always did when he had something on his mind. Finally he said, "I've been thinking about the lights and night noises out on the bay that Stanley was supposed to be raving about. Maybe he saw something similar to what Juan came across."

I said, "What do you think they were doing? Smuggling? That must have been it, and it would account for the secrecy and the attack on Juan."

Mack said, "It could have been marijuana, packages of cocaine. My bet is some kind of illegal drugs. There could be a natural pipeline into Brooklyn, Queens, even the high schools in Nassau and Suffolk County. Remember that airplane that was seized at the Easthampton Airport a couple of years ago? They were carrying a fortune in cocaine."

He thought for a moment, then added, "It's just like the old days, during Prohibition, when the rum runners plied the waters of Long Island."

"Let's see what we can find on the internet," I said.

My initial search came up with several items of interest, both from the *New York Times*. The first announced that a drug patrol was planned for the Long Island shores. It read, in part, "For the first time, federal authorities have begun operating undercover high-speed patrol boats and aircraft from Long Island to try to intercept drug-laden vessels heading for the Island's shoreline. In recent weeks the new unmarked craft, a sport fishing yacht and two racing boats, a helicopter, and an airplane, have begun to bring to New York waters the tactics often used to catch drug smugglers in southern Florida."

The other article was a bit of a let down, considering its relation to the first: "Coast Guard on Long Island Faces Budget Cut." The article went on to say that due to cuts in Homeland Security, the proposed budget for the Coast Guard could cause major problems on Long Island, especially in battling drug smuggling. One Coast Guard base had been closed, and the other facilities were stretched thin, covering miles of coastline.

A further search revealed another article, announcing that the U.S. Customs Service had seized 1,100 pounds of cocaine on Long Island. The estimated street value of the cocaine is $120 million. The agent-in-charge said, "Our investigation uncovered a narcotics smuggling work in progress, a drug distribution cell disguised as a respectable landscaping business in the heart of suburbia."

Mack related a conversation he overheard at the barbershop, where a local mortician was holding forth about another drug smuggling plot. It seems that an undertaker in Brooklyn had made an arrangement with his cousin in Palermo, who was in the same business. When a body was consigned to be sent back to the Italian homeland, the American cousin would pack the sealed lead coffin with cocaine and ship it to his counterpart in Italy. Drug-sniffing dogs could not detect the cocaine, and as a rule, sealed coffins are not inspected in customs.

Mack said, "That's an interesting concept, using a legitimate business as a front. About those so-called clam diggers that Juan saw. I wonder if Leroy Kemp knows what his kids are up to?"

I said, "I think we should pay a visit to Leroy."

Chapter 17

"If I had my way, no man guilty of golf would be eligible to any office of trust under the United States." —H.L. Mencken

While Leroy Kemp and I had taught and coached in the same school, we never did see eye to eye. I did not like his coaching methods, and I'm sure he didn't approve of mine. First, he would let an athlete play hurt, and as a result, a number of his players wound up with bad knees for life. His philosophy was to win at any cost, and he had racked up an impressive record of victories during his career. In fact, the football field had been named after him. In spite of all the league championships, one title eluded him all his life: coach of the year. I think the sportswriters and coaches who voted for the award were trying to tell him something.

As we drove along the street that led to Kemp's house, we saw a succession of signs, reading, "Leroy knows football," "Leroy knows kids," "Leroy knows education," and the last one, "Leroy Kemp for School Board."

"That's a laugh," I said. "I remember Leroy's health classes. The only thing he did was show old football movies, instead of talking about sex education and nutrition."

Mack said, "Those who can't do, teach; those who can't teach, run for the school board."

Leroy's house was an imposing edifice overlooking the bay, with a sweeping driveway and white columns in the front. Mack said, "I guess Leroy is doing all right for himself these days. This is some setup."

I replied, "How could he afford a place like this on a school teacher's salary, even with the coaching differential?"

Mack said, "Well, his wife works in real estate. Maybe she helped out with the price tag."

I thought about real estate for a moment. Carol had been taking courses recently, and had educated me a little. Even with the recent depression in real estate sales, the prices of houses on Long Island were incredibly inflated. We had bought a house in the fifties, getting almost two acres for $15,000. That same piece of property, fifty years later or so, was priced at $500,000.

We parked the car and walked up to the entrance of the mini-mansion. I rang the bell, and chimes sounded somewhere inside the house. After a few minutes, an imposing blonde opened the door. It was Mrs. Kemp.

Her face was flushed, and her voice sounded as if it had seen too many cigarettes.

"Yes?" she said, in an imperious tone, as if we had interrupted an important meeting.

Mack turned on the charm. "Hi, Ms. Kemp. I don't know if you remember us, Mack Thomas and Sal Cascio. We used to work with your husband at the high school. Is he in?"

The woman stared at Mack, frowned as if she was trying to clear her head, then bellowed in a loud voice, "Lee-Roy! Lee-roy! Someone's here to see you!"

A voice roared from a back room, "What? Who is it? I wasn't expecting anybody."

I wondered if these two spent their days shouting at each other. Maybe it had to do with the size of the house.

Soon a body appeared to match the voice. Leroy had put on a bit of weight since retirement. We had heard that he was still coaching, and turning over his coaching salary to his assistants, but he hadn't stayed in shape. As he walked towards us, an amazing transformation took place: his face brightened, his eyes sparkled, and he strode towards us with a smile and a hand extended.

"Hey, how you guys doin'? I haven't seen you since, I don't know when. Whatcha been up to?"

Mack said, "Leroy, we wondered if we could talk."

Leroy said, "Sure. No problem. You want to find out about my campaign? I sure could use your support. A lot of the teachers respect you guys."

He escorted us into a spacious living room, filled with expensive looking leather furniture. There was a trophy cabinet, appropriately lit, and the walls were covered with plaques and testimonials to the coach's career.

Mack said, "Actually, Leroy, we just found out you were running for the board. No, we wanted to talk to you about something else."

"What's that?"

Mack said, "Well, we wanted to know if you were still running that clamming operation for the kids."

Leroy frowned, as if he had come across a bad smell, and said, "Naw, I haven't had anything to do with that for a couple of years now. I think some of the older guys kept it going, though. They must be in college by now. Why are you asking about that?"

Mack said, "We heard that some of them were clamming in restricted waters, going out at night, stuff like that."

Leroy said, "No, my boys wouldn't do anything like that. I taught them right, you know."

I bet you did, I thought to myself.

Meanwhile, Mrs. Kemp had entered the room, and walked over to a bar, saying, "Anybody want a drink?"

Leroy frowned, and said, "We're talkin' here, Mae."

Mack and I declined her offer, though a Scotch would have hit the spot for me.

Mack said, "Can you think of any one who might be involved in using the clamming business as a front for some kind of illegal activity?"

Leroy glared at us, and said, "I don't know what you're talking about. And if I hear about you guys spreading that shit around town, you will have a lawsuit on your hands. Now, I think our conversation is over."

Chapter 18

"Golf is very much like a love affair. If you don't take it seriously, it's no fun; if you do, it breaks your heart."
—Louise Suggs

Shortly after Juan was released from the hospital, Maria and Mack were having dinner at the local pizza parlor. Over brick oven pizzas, they talked about what had happened.

Maria said, "Have you and Sal found out why Juan was attacked and left for dead?"

Mack said, "Not really. We have our suspicions, but no tangible proof. We don't even know who did it, but we have a general idea."

"Why have you not reported these things to the police?" she asked.

Mack said, "Well, as I said, we have no proof. And given Juan's recent unpleasantness with the authorities, they might not take us seriously."

Maria's cheeks reddened, and she said angrily, "When we came to this country, we thought we were getting away from all the violence, and the lack of justice. Now it is just as bad as before."

Mack said, "Well, we don't have death squads and a corrupt government. At least not yet, in spite of the general terrorist paranoia. But I can understand how you must feel."

A few days later, Maria called Mack from work. Voice shaking, in tears, she said, "Mack, I must see you at once. Something terrible has happened."

Mack rushed over to the hospice, and was met at the door by Maria. She held an envelope out to Mack with a shaking hand.

Mack pulled out a folded piece of paper and opened it. Printed in crude letters in magic marker were the words, "Wetback, go home—if you know what's good for you!"

Maria said, in fear and anger, "This came to the house. It was addressed to Juan, but he did not see it. I found it in the mailbox, but it has no stamp."

She added, "Mack, someone knows Juan survived the attack in the water, and that person wants to make sure he doesn't go to the authorities."

Mack put his arms around Maria, and said, "Don't worry, darlin'. Sal and I will figure out what to do. Let's all get together tonight and figure out a plan, something that's safe for you and Juan."

Later that day, we had a cookout. It was early evening, and there was the pop, twist, and chatter of lawn sprinklers trying to beat the heat back from dying lawns. There was the ubiquitous sound of an ice cream truck in the distance, and in a nearby strip mall, teenagers on skateboards were rolling with clamorous thunder. As Juan and the twins splashed in the shallow end of the pool, we talked about the best plan of action to take. Maria wanted to go to the authorities, and Carol agreed with her. Carol said, "We can't let them get away with this kind of thing. This is America, for goodness' sake."

Sal said, "You're right, Carol. But the problem is we don't know who 'they' are. We couldn't get anything out of Kemp. He stonewalled us for sure."

Mack flipped a couple of hamburgers over, then said, "I still think we should talk to him again. Maybe find some way to put the pressure on him."

"I agree," Sal said, "but we need a little time to develop something. Meanwhile, how do we keep Juan and Maria out of harm's way?"

Mack thought for a few minutes as he finished the burgers and prepared to serve them. As we all sat down to dinner, he said, "I think I've figured out what to do. You know those friends of ours who live down in Florida, the ones with the horse ranch north of Orlando?"

Mack was referring to Dan and Belle Laybourne. Dan was a retired airline pilot and Belle was a world-class tennis player with a love for quarter horses. They had about 200 horses on their ranch in Minnesota, and usually brought two or three favorites down to Florida in the winter, along with six dogs and a number of cats.

Mack said, "Every time we have visited them, there's a lot of work that needs to be done, mending fences, cutting brush, repair on the house, that kind of thing. Juan could be a great help to Dan, especially since he's recovering from another bypass."

"We wouldn't want to be too much trouble to them," Maria said.

Mack laughed, "They would be glad to have you. They're the kind of generous, open-hearted people who would take in any stray that showed up at their door. And if one of those strays was a strong, young buck like Juan, willing to work, they would be doubly glad to see him. They could use the company of a nurse, too, Maria, since they both have had bypass surgery in the last year."

Chapter 19

"It took me seventeen years to get 3,000 hits in baseball. I did it in one afternoon on the golf course." —Hank Aaron

A week later, we packed up my car and drove Juan and Maria to Lorton, Virginia, where we caught the Amtrak car train for Sanford, Florida, not far from the lake district and the winding maze of unmarked back roads leading to the compound owned by our friends Dan and Belle. We had decided to take the car train because it was a less obvious way to get Juan and Maria down to Florida, especially if someone were watching the airport. As I had anticipated, Dan and Belle welcomed us with open arms, and seemed especially glad to have house guests for a month or so, especially a strong, young man to help Dan with the maintenance of the place. With an electric gate and the pack of dogs roaming the place, the compound seemed almost impregnable. On top of that, Dan had a collection of rifles and shotguns, and was a proficient marksman with military training.

The night before we returned to New York, we sat down over a meal at a local fish camp. Even that place was on a remote lake, and there were more airboats than cars parked around the restaurant, if you could call it that.

Dan said, "I'm sorry you and Mack have to head back to New York. As usual, your stay is too short."

I replied, "That's because you want more work out of me, Dan."

We had spent the afternoon planting young palm trees, weighing about 600 pounds each, and my back was going to take a month to recover.

Mack said, "That's because my sedentary friend is spending too much time in front of the computer, and not enough time in the gym."

"Well, somebody has got to do the research and pay the bills," I answered.

Juan said, "Is it true, Señor Dan, that gator bits taste like fried chicken?"

The next day, Mack and I returned to Long Island. As we drove into Southport, we saw a column of black smoke rising from the direction of the marina. We arrived at the marina in time to watch the local fire department extinguishing the blaze in a 26-foot boat called the "Bay Runner." I knew the chief as we had been probies together 25 years ago. He had continued with the department, and I had to resign after my knees began to trouble me, but we still would share a beer or two in the department's recreation room.

As he came off the dock, I met him with the universal firefighter's greeting, "George, how ya' doin'?"

He answered, "Hi, Sal. That was some cooker. One of the boats next to the fire was burned, but we managed to save the one on the other side."

I said, "Whose boat was it, George?"

He said, "That was Leroy Kemp's boat. You know, the guy running for the school board."

"What do you think caused the fire?" I said.

"The dock master said he was always after him to turn the electrical breakers off, but he left them on all the time. That could have been it. But the county arson squad just got here, and maybe they will find something else, like a little 'insurance lightning,' something like that."

I had the feeling that Kemp was not going to get the chief's vote in the upcoming school board election.

One of the things you learn in the private investigation business is that there are very few coincidences. The burning of Kemp's boat, the one he probably used in his clamming ventures, so soon after we had tried to talk to him, was a coincidence not to be ignored.

The next thing that surprised us shortly after our return from Florida was the news in the *Long Island Business Weekly* that the Treasure Oak Golf Course and Country Club was being sold to the Island Treasure Corporation, an outfit that specialized in high-end golf resort/ retirement communities. For the purchase price of $500,000 and an annual membership-maintenance fee of only $50,000, residents could be assured of exclusive golf privileges with no waiting in line, and without having to rub up against the unwashed louts who clutter the public courses.

"I guess the Japanese decided they were not welcome," Mack said.

We decided we needed to find out about the new owners.

Chapter 20

"Golf is a spiritual game. It's like Zen. You have to let your mind take over." —Amy Strum Alcott

Such matters as new real estate developments were far removed from our minds the next day, for we were embroiled in one of the deeply philosophical discussions that can accompany a round of golf.

Mack said, "You son of a bitch, I think you hit my ball!"

He was furious, for he had just spent five minutes in the rough, looking for his drive. Finally, he had reluctantly taken a penalty stroke, and dropped a new ball onto the fairway.

I answered, "What are you crying about now? What are you playing?"

"A Pinnacle 2. I told you that when we started…"

I said, "Stop whining. You better hit your approach shot. The ranger looks as if he wants to talk to us."

Sure enough, Gus, the retiree who worked as a starter and ranger, was driving towards us on a golf cart. Clearly nettled, my partner rushed to hit his approach shot, sending a line drive into a bunker the size of the Sahara. I expressed my insincere condolences, then watched my perfectly hit ball climb lazily, with just the right amount of fade, then drop and run to within a few feet of the cup. As we drove towards the green, I said, "Shouldn't gnash your teeth, partner, you haven't got that many working ones left."

"I could concentrate better if you didn't smoke those foul Italian cigars," Mack grumbled.

Gus, the starter, finally reached us as we finished our putts. He said, "There's a cop waiting for you at the clubhouse, said he wanted to see you right away."

Mack said, "Is he one of the local boys?"

Gus answered, "No, I think he's county. They have been investigating the dead guy they found on the ninth hole this morning."

"What dead guy?" I asked.

"The guy lying on the green two holes ahead of you," he said.

As far as I'm concerned, death on a golf course in the middle of a beautiful sunny day is bad manners. It's out of place, like laughing at a funeral or farting in church. For a while, play had continued on the course; however, a log jam was building as we and the players behind us came on the scene. Some of the players stood around, swinging golf clubs, nervously lighting cigarettes, talking in muted tones. Someone asked, "Do you think he would mind if we played through?" Nobody laughed, not even me.

A county police car appeared, bouncing and swerving down the service road that snaked its way throughout the course. In the distance, there was the wail of an ambulance siren.

Alonzo Fagan, the detective from the Fifth Precinct, was clearly not happy with finding a body with a nine iron in its head on the ninth green. Unwittingly, he fit the stereotype of most detectives in crime fiction: short haircut, no facial hair, polyester pants and tie, checked jacket. In his eyes there was that basic resentment that most civil employees feel for teachers who only work 180 days a year.

Contrary to the local constabulary, with whom we had a good working relationship, I got the strong feeling that the county police department considered themselves too professional to deal with the likes of a couple of amateur gumshoes. He was also not looking forward to interviewing dozens of possible witnesses.

After his fifteenth interview, I got the impression that the detective was clearly growing impatient with us. He was obviously one of those individuals who thought golf as a stupid game, played by grown men in silly outfits, chasing a little white pellet for five hours at a time in the broiling sun. He said, "I find it difficult to believe that nobody saw anything, heard anything, in the middle of a crowded golf course." As if to punctuate his remarks, he paused and surveyed the surrounding area.

The course was built around a large pond referred to by geologists as a kettle, formed thousands of years ago when a huge piece of ice had fallen from a receding glacier. To the east of the golf course, twenty acres of tall pines stood in silent testimony to what had once been a great forest decimated by wood cutters from Connecticut. There were many shrubs and trees on the course, some bordering on the fanciful, for it had been carved out of an old tree nursery owned by a sea captain turned husbandry man, an amateur botanist who returned from his voyages with all kinds of strange and exotic flora. It was the kind of wooded course where players had to hit a straight drive or else, for at many points, thick growths of trees encroached the fairways from both sides, forming narrow bottlenecks. Stands of bamboo surrounded the water holes, flowering crab apple and tulip trees bordered the fairways, and each tee was lined with thick covering of white oak and evergreens, which effectively muffled the rude shouts and occasional grunts and curses of nearby golfers. For that reason, nobody had been able to see a murderer sink a nine iron in the skull of Stanley's hapless brother.

Mack said, "I will bet you my grandmother's rocking chair that this is connected with Stanley's death and the money he had in the bank." I saluted him for stating the blatantly obvious.

At that point, Detective Fagan got around to us. "All right, you two, what have you got to say for yourselves?"

Evidently he meant to interview us as a team, contrary to police procedure.

He looked up at Mack, who towered over him by a foot or two, and said, "Your name Thomas?"

"Yes, it is. Any problem, officer?"

"Ya gotta license?"

Mack said, "No, I don't have a driver's license. Haven't had one for many years, in fact."

Fagan looked as if he was about to hit Mack. "Don't be a wise guy," he said. "You know what I mean. Your PI license."

"I don't have it yet. I'm still waiting…"

"Whatta ya mean?" As Fagan spoke, curiously, his lips didn't seem to move at all.

"What I mean, officer, is that my license has been approved, but I haven't gotten the piece of paper from the state. Don't worry, I'm legitimate."

The angry detective stepped back and looked at us for a moment. Then he said, "I got two murders I'm working on, this guy and his brother. And every time I talk to someone, I find out some half-assed schoolteacher has been there first. Look, guys, why dontcha leave the police work to the pros? Stick to divorces and insurance stuff. You keep getting' in my way, you're gonna wish you stayed in the classroom."

He turned away from us, then spun around, spitting his words out, "Besides, we got a lead on old Stanley you smart asses don't even know about."

Chapter 21

"Give me golf clubs, fresh air, and a beautiful partner, and you can keep the clubs and the fresh air." —Jack Benny

Later that week, Mack and I were following a late-model car driven by a man in a neck brace. As usual, I was driving, and Mack held held a camcorder at the ready.

Mack said, "I thought this guy claimed he couldn't do anything."

"He looks pretty chipper to me," I said. "Are you sure you know how to use that thing? I'm giving up a good ball game just to do you a favor, and you won't even let me smoke!"

Mack said, "Quit grousing, will you? Tell you what, when we finish, I'll get you a pack of those El Stinkos you like so much."

I pulled over to the side of the road as the car we were following stopped in front of a bowling alley. Mack turned the camera on, then grunted with satisfaction as the subject of our investigation opened the trunk of his car, removed his neck brace, and grabbed his bowling bag. Mack hooted, "Man, the insurance company is going to give us an Academy Award for this one!"

As we pulled away, the conversation turned to our other investigations, most of which were not going anywhere. Stanley and his brother, the departing Japanese, Leroy Kemp and his clam diggers, Juan's attackers: each one was like a nagging toothache that wouldn't go away. Mack said, "I can't help but think that they are related in some way, but how?"

I said, "Maybe we should follow Leroy for a couple of days, see who he talks to."

Mack said, "That's crazy. He's running for the school board. He's all over town, talking to anybody who will listen to him. I heard he did a special mailing to all his old football players and their parents, asking them for their vote and a five dollar donation to his campaign."

"Now, that takes chutzpah," I said.

Later that evening, we sat on the deck behind Mack's house, drinking Cokes and talking about our various cases. It was a night for sitting out. Warring fireflies sent tracers through the darkness. Horseshoes rang in the nearby park in raucous counterpoint to the pop and hiss of opening soda cans and the occasional thoughtful belch.

Mack said, "I've been thinking about Leroy. Maybe he won't talk to us, but I'll bet his wife will. I hear she spends a lot of time at the country club bar. Maybe we should buy her a drink and see what she has to say."

"Now that's a mean, low-down scheme, taking advantage of a lush," I said, "but you're right, it's probably the best idea you've had all day."

The next day, we played a round of golf in the morning, then headed to the club for lunch. As we sat over corned beef sandwiches and sodas, we saw Mae Kemp enter the club with a tall, slender brunette.

I said, "Who's the babe? She's a real looker."

Mack answered, "I don't know, but she might make our job a little easier. It might look funny if two guys were offering to buy a lady a drink."

We walked over to their table, and Mack asked, "Hello, ladies, mind if we join you for a few minutes? Buy you a drink?"

At the sound of the word 'drink,' Mae Kemp's face turned from a frown to a smile. She smiled even wider when Mack added, "Mae, we understand you're in real estate, and we have some questions for you. Sal here wants to sell his house, you know."

At this last piece of news, both women looked at each other and smiled, as visions of commissions danced before their eyes.

The other woman turned out to be no other than Mary Alice Jones, Mae's mentor and partner in the real estate business. While Mack went to the bar to get their drinks, the women turned their heated gaze on me. "Where is your house, Sal," asked Mary Alice.

When I told them that my humble abode was across the street from a National Wildlife Refuge and about a quarter of a mile from the water, you would have said that I was offering the Taj Mahal at bargain basement prices. Their breathing became heavy, and I'm sure it wasn't my Mediterranean sex appeal.

Mae reached over, put her hand on my arm, and looked into my eyes feverishly.

"Sal, I'm so sorry that you're leaving town. Is that what you're doing? Moving south like so many retired teachers?"

At that moment, Mack returned with their drinks, and sat down, saying, "Yes, Sal wants to get out of town right away. But I'm sure he will still be here for the school board election."

Mae snorted, "Oh, that old thing. I don't know why Leroy wants to be on the school board. All those nights out, with late meetings. I don't know what I'm going to do with myself."

I said, "Maybe you need to take up a hobby, like golf."

Chapter 22

"Golf is not just exercise; it is an adventure, a romance, a Shakespearean play in which disaster and comedy are intertwined." —Harold Segall

Our conversation with Mae and Mary Alice revealed several interesting items. Evidently Leroy was telling the truth about getting out of the clamming business. Why he got out was another story. He told his wife he had made a killing in the stock market (we wondered about that choice of words) and didn't need to work any more. We also learned that like many before him, he saw the school board as a stepping stone to further political aspirations. He had mentioned to her the notion of running for mayor of the village the next year, then maybe town council the following. They say that power is a drug, and it appeared to us that Leroy was hooked. These plans were more than enough motivation to shut the clamming business down and remove himself as far as possible from any illegal activity related to it.

Meanwhile, the school board election was getting nasty. Leroy's opponent, Marcie Malone, published a letter to the editor of the local weekly newspaper, complaining that someone had been defacing and taking down her campaign signs, which were few in number compared to the barrage of Leroy for School Board signs that had sprung up all over the district. Marcie couldn't prove anything, but someone was doing the dirty work, and it just wasn't fair. Moreover, she had been getting nasty phone calls late at night, and the final insult, her mailbox had been bashed by someone in a pickup truck.

In the same issue, the editorial called for a clean school board campaign, forcefully arguing that such dirty tricks were more in the purview of presidential elections.

There was a meet the candidate night coming up, and Mack said he planned to attend it. I decided to go too, in case he needed a bodyguard.

The meeting was held in the auditorium of the local junior high school, and was playing to a full house, which seemed to hold a large number of ex-football players. There were three candidates sitting on the stage: Leroy, Ms. Malone, and Joe Hendrix, a scientist from Brookhaven Lab who had served on the board for a number of years. The editor of the local newspaper was the moderator, and once he got the crowd settled down, laid out the ground rules.

He said, "First we will have statements from each of the candidates, lasting no more than ten minutes each. Then each candidate will have an additional ten minutes to respond to anything his or her opponent says. Then we will have questions from the audience."

Hendrix spoke first. His platform was one of continued dedication to the students, to improving test scores, of quality performance by teachers. When he sat down, there was polite applause, as well as a few catcalls and whistles from the football crowd.

Ms. Malone was next, clearly nervous and a bit intimidated by the audience. She started her speech, then apparently lost her place and stumbled over a few words. At that, the Kemp faction burst out laughing, and there were more whistles and catcalls. "What's the matter, lady, lost your place?"

"Sit down if you got nothin' else to say!"

Ms. Malone was finally able to finish her statement, much to her credit. Then Kemp stood up amidst thundering applause from his young supporters.

"O.K. boys, now settle down. This is supposed to be a dignified occasion, haw, haw." There was more applause.

Kemp said, "You all know me and what I believe in. I believe in hard work, that real sweat and effort pays off, and not just in championship football teams. (applause) I think we can provide quality education for our teams and students without raising taxes, contrary what my opponents think. I think we should do away with teacher tenure, and get rid of some of the dead wood on the faculty. We have teachers who work a hundred and eighty days, and make over $100,000 a year. If we get rid of the old timers, we can hire two or three young teachers to take their place for the same cost." (more applause)

"Finally, we need to cut down on administrative costs. We have too many assistant superintendents of this and that, all making hundreds of thousands a year. We don't need all those people, many of whom have never seen the inside of a classroom."

Leroy went on in this vein for his allotted ten minutes, then sat down to thunderous applause.

The moderator stood up and said, "Now we will have questions from the audience."

Mack stood up, and the moderator said, "Please state your name before you ask a question or make a statement."

"My name is Mckinley Thomas, and I used to teach at the high school. I was one of those high-priced teachers that only worked a hundred and eighty days a year."

This statement was followed by applause and a few catcalls, probably from students who had failed Mack's class.

Mack said, "I have a question for the candidates regarding our athletic budget, which appears to be rather inflated. We spend thousands of dollars every year on about a hundred athletes on our varsity teams, while the rest of the student body, which consists of about 1,500 overweight youngsters, gets no athletic activity except one or two gym classes of 40 minutes each per week. No wonder there is an epidemic of obesity among our youth. My question is this: If elected, will you institute an after school intramural sports program, giving every student in the school the opportunity for regular exercise in such lifetime sports as tennis?"

Mack's question brought a chorus of derisive shouts from the football players, and a smattering of applause from many adults in the audience.

Kemp stood up, his face flushed, and said in an angry tone, "Let me ask Mr. Thomas a question. Who's going to pay for the cost of the intramural program?"

"We would have to take money out of the athletic budget for that."

Mack retorted, "Yes, you might not be able to buy new uniforms every year, Leroy, but do the math. Shouldn't our sports budget benefit every kid in the school, and not just a select few?"

You would think that Mack was preaching heresy, considering the mounting chorus of abuse from the football faction.

Then it was my turn. I stood up and was recognized by the moderator. "Mr. Cascio, is it? Weren't you the wrestling coach at the school?"

Some of the football players, graduates who also had wrestled on my team, evidently expected me to rebut Mack's position.

I said, "Is it true, Mr. Kemp, that you plan to run for the office of mayor next year, and don't you think we could be looking at a conflict of interest here?"

My question clearly shook Leroy. He said, "I-I don't know what you're talking about, Sal."

There was a buzz in the audience, as people looked at each other in puzzlement. "What is he talking about? Mayor? I thought this was a school board election."

I sat down next to Mack, and the way Leroy and his legion of louts glared at us, you would think we were in trouble.

After the meeting, we went out to the parking lot, only to find that I had a flat tire. On closer inspection, I found that one of my tires had been slashed.

"I should have ridden my bike," said Mack.

Chapter 23

"Golf is a fine relief from the tensions of office, but we are a little tired of holding the bag." —Adlai Stevenson

A day or so later, Mack got off the phone and pumped his arm in a victory gesture. "What's that for?" I said.

"We've got an appointment with the County police."

"I thought they didn't like us," I said.

Mack answered, "I just got off the phone with Gus Hightower. I decided to pull an end run around our friend Detective Fagan. Gus said he just got the medical examiner's reports on Stanley and his brother."

Augustus Hightower was a captain in the county police force who taught forensics at the police academy. He and Mack had become friends when Mack invited him to speak to his students during his crime and punishment unit. His tales of medical examinations and bizarre killings brought added interest to Mack's reading assignments in Dosteovsky and Sir Arthur Conan Doyle. He also arranged for Mack's students to tour the county jail, and I am sure those visits kept many a potential delinquent from going down the drain.

When we entered his office later that day, I was struck by his appearance. He had white hair in a very close crew cut, probably cropped once a week. He was freshly shaved, with smooth, pink cheeks that glowed with health. He wore a natty sports jacket, and small, beady eyes peered out from folds of flesh around his eyes. He reminded me of a muscular turtle.

A punching bag hung in the corner of the room, and a glass case nearby was filled with amateur boxing trophies. The captain was clearly not a person to be messed with.

At that point, Detective Fagan entered the room. He said, "I thought I saw these two come in here. Cap, these are the two bozos I told you about. Couple of school teachers playing detective."

Captain Hightower was clearly annoyed at the intrusion, but said calmly, "Detective Fagan, these gentlemen are here as my guests, and I would appreciate it if you treated them accordingly. Now, what can I do for you?"

Fagan seemed to choke on something, swallowed, then left the room.

The Captain sat there for a moment, then said, "Cascio. I know you. Used to go to all the home matches. You had some pretty tough teams, small but scrappy. Had some wild fights after the matches."

"Yeah, until the Board of Ed wised up and agreed to a daytime schedule. The problem with night matches wasn't the kids, it was all the rednecks and drunks from town."

Captain Hightower said, "Well, you may be right. But we've got more important business at hand, and we should do it by the book."

At this, he pressed a buzzer on his desk, and said, "Sally, come in here, will you, and bring your steno pad."

As the stenographer took notes, the captain started the questioning, directing most of them at Mack. "State your name, age, address, please."

"Macintosh Thomas, age 64, 142 Golf Course Drive, Southport."

"Profession?"

"Retired history teacher, Southport Schools, currently working as a private investigator."

"How many years as a private investigator?"

"Two. I'm just getting started."

"License?"

"I was told over the phone a few months ago that it was approved.

I don't have the piece of paper, as I told Detective Fagan, but that's New York State for you. The land of taxes and red tape."

"What kind of work have you been doing?"

"Mostly insurance fraud and cable TV rip-offs."

"For who?"

"Suburbia Cable and Royal Fire and Casualty."

"Our computer says you have a string of traffic violations and a number of accidents. I'm surprised you got a license. How do you get around?"

"That's where I come in," I said.

The captain said, "So you're the driver, and, I take it, his partner in crime."

"Sometimes it feels like it. Most of the time, he can't do anything without me. You should see him on the golf course. Half the time, he doesn't even know which club to use."

The captain smiled, then said, "O.K. Let's get serious. How come you guys are involved in this thing with Stanley and his brother, whose name, by the way, is Henry."

I said, "I guess I'm the one to blame. I grew up around here, and remember Stanley from when I was a kid. He used to take me fishing, and showed me the best places to go crabbing. I remember a lot of happy hours with the old guy, and when I heard he had been killed, it made me madder than hell."

Mack said, "Since we are emotionally involved in this matter, it occurred to us that we could work cooperatively. We promise to tell you everything we find out, as soon as we find it."

The captain thought for a moment, then said, "You guys got moxie, I'll give you that. Tell you what, if I give you the preliminary results of the medical examiner's report, will you guys promise to stay out of our way?"

Mack put on his most humble face and said, "Yeah, sure thing. We'd love to see you guys clear this thing up. We were talking about getting back to our routine stuff anyway, the business that pays the bills."

The captain said, "Well, that's a good thing. Now, where did I put that report?" He rummaged around the papers on his desk, then came up with an official-looking document. He started to read: "Let's see. Dr. Abdul Rezza, Forensic Pathologist, July 15, 3:00 p.m…a lot of technical stuff…" He looked up, then said, "The long and short of it is that Stanley and his brother were killed with the same gun."

Mack gave a start, "Same gun? I thought he was killed with a nine iron."

"Well, that helped, but the medical examiner said the initial cause of death was a bullet to the heart, a.30-.30 rifle bullet, to be exact. The nine iron was for effect, I guess."

Chapter 24

"Playing golf is like chasing a pill around a cow pasture."
—*Winston Churchill*

Journal entry: "Leroy Kemp won the school board race!"

I still find that hard to believe. His victory is a sad commentary on the fickleness of the public, who obviously chose to vote with their wallets and not their intellect. Then again, when I think of all those years of winning teams and adoring parents, Kemp had developed quite a following, a claque that translated into a lot of votes. What's next? Mayor? Congressman? Stranger things have happened. Let's face it, we tend to idolize our sports heroes. High school athletes, especially football players, are the center of attraction. I should know. I played football in high school, and got the attention of the captain of the cheerleading squad. The pleasure of her company was worth all the hours of practice, the sweat and the pain of butting heads with other hormone-driven young men.

According to Mae, Kemp is spending more time away from home than before, and when he is at home, he must deal with a weekly pile of reports and other reading matter to prepare for each meeting. If school board candidates knew how much homework they had, I'm sure many would decide not to run. Mae has taken up golf in earnest, and on several occasions, she and her friend Mary Alice have joined us in playing mixed doubles.

Mae Kemp has turned out to be a natural athlete, and hits the ball with a certain ferocity that suggests she is aiming at her husband's head. On one such occasion, we learned from her that Leroy had been on the course the day of Henry's death.

We wondered if a nine iron was missing from his bag, but didn't find the occasion to pose that question.

On one such outing, when Mary Alice was working her charms on me, trying to get a commitment about selling my house, Mack brought up the subject of Henry's death.

He said, "Mae, isn't it terrible what happened on this course a while ago?"

She said, "What do you mean, Mack?"

"You know, when they found that fellow on the ninth green, with a club in his head. It turned out later that someone had shot him first."

"Oh, that's so awful, I don't like to think about it. Leroy was on the course that day, but he didn't want to talk about it, and I'm glad he didn't."

As an afterthought, she added, "He was playing with one of the Gonzago brothers."

The Gonzago brothers were twins with identical crew cuts, broad shoulders, lean hips, and a feral gleam in their eyes. When it came to football, it seemed that they had a license to maim the opponents. Eric Gonzaga played linebacker, and Anthony played defensive end. They were a lethal combination. Anthony had a reputation for using his hands as battering rams during a pile up, and Eric specialized in spearing runners, aiming his helmet in the center of their chest, a practice supposedly banned in high school football. Coach Kemp tended to look the other way during such play, and was outraged if the officials started penalizing the twins.

The twins also were part of Leroy's clam digging enterprise, and they must have made a lot of money, for they drove a pair of matching Hummers. Moreover, we saw them working out at the local gym when the rest of the world went off to legitimate, 9 to 5 jobs. According to Mae, the Gonzagos would also go upstate with Leroy on hunting trips, and were crack shots.

We also learned that one of the twins, Anthony, had recently taken a job as a groundskeeper on the golf course. I guess with the price of gas going up so high, he had to do something to feed his four-wheeled monster.

So Kemp and the Gonzago twins were all on the same course when Henry was killed. Mack said, "This is too big a coincidence to be ignored, but we're still lacking a motive."

"Why would they want Henry dead?" I asked.

Mack thought for a while, then said, "You talked to Henry that day, when you accosted him on the golf course. How did he seem to you? Nervous? Worried?"

I said, "No, but he was upset about Stanley."

Mack said, "Where was Henry staying? With anybody?"

"No, I think he said he was living in the marsh house."

Mack said, "I think we should take a look at the marsh house. Maybe we'll find some clues."

Chapter 25

"If there is any larceny in a man, golf will bring it out."
—*Paul Gallico*

Later that day, Mack and I slogged through the reeds, following a muddy path to the marsh house. Startled by our approach, a flock of ducks took flight, their wings flapping indignantly. It was a warm day, and muskrats scrambled away through the weeds. As we neared the mash house, the bottle garden glistened in the sunlight. Mack said, "That's some collection of bottles. I guess Stanley liked his drink."

I said, "Yeah. Looks like mostly wine and beer."

We climbed up the ramp that led to the entrance of the run-down shack. As we pushed the door open, we were met with the smell of unwashed clothing and bedding, and the rank odor of spoiled food. The place looked like a hurricane had hit it, with books and furniture strewn everywhere. The wood stove had been knocked over, and ashes spread across the floor.

I said, "Looks like someone got here before we did, or maybe it was just kids raising hell."

Mack said, "No, I think it looks like someone was looking for something."

He picked up one of the books and shook his head. "It's a shame. They even tore some of the pages out of the books."

Mack then said, "Think hard. Did Henry say anything about

Stanley? He must have stayed here for a couple of weeks before he was killed. Maybe he found something in Stanley's stuff."

"Yeah," I answered, "and maybe he hid it. And I'll bet that's what got him killed."

"Well, whoever killed Stanley did not know he had a brother, and probably got nervous when Henry showed up and stayed in the marsh house."

I said, "Do we agree that they were killed by the same person, or persons? After all, the same kind of bullet, the money in the bank, all that?"

Mack said, "It's mostly circumstantial, but logic sometimes leads to interesting conclusions."

As we left the marsh house, Mack stopped and looked at the bottle garden. He said, "Funny, whoever was here must have been art lovers. They didn't disturb the bottle garden."

I looked at the bottles more closely. I had never really studied the pattern or arrangement. The bottles were arranged in a loose, concentric circle, starting with smaller bottles on the outside, and working towards larger ones on the inside. The bottles were brown, clear, or green, and the colors were worked to create a pattern that made the whole arrangement look like a glass bull's eye.

Mack said, "I wonder if Stanley arranged the bottles that way for a reason."

I answered, "Maybe there was a method to his madness, like he was trying to leave a message."

At that moment, Mack picked up the centermost bottle, a large green wine bottle, and exclaimed, "There's something in this bottle. Look!"

The bottle had been stopped up with a cork, and inside there was something that looked like a rolled up piece of paper.

Chapter 26

"Golf courses are the best places to observe ministers, but none of them are above cheating a bit." —*John D. Rockefeller*

The bottle at the center of Stanley's garden was not empty. Pulling out the cork, I shook the bottle, and a tightly-rolled piece of paper with a rubber band around it fell to the ground. Mack picked it up and looked at it.

The piece of paper turned out to be a crudely drawn map. The handwriting was a childish scrawl. In the center of the map was an X, and a wavering, dotted line led from that mark to the shore of Great South Bay. It looked like an old pirate's map, drawn with a magic marker. Next to the X were the words "Old Oak Tree." In the bay, there was a drawing of a small island with the words "Robins Island."

I said, "This old oak tree must be near the golf course."

Mack said, "There aren't that many oak trees left on that part of the island. The people who developed the golf course cut down most of the trees, and the last hurricane took down a lot more. But there must be one or two still standing."

I said, "Why don't we go and take a look?"

On the road leading to the course there was a new sign, which read: "Coming soon! Treasure Oak Condominiums. Exclusive golf villas, starting at $500,000. Free membership, country club privileges."

"That's new," Mack said.

"And a little out of our price range," I added. "Maybe that's why the Japanese were 'encouraged' to leave."

"What do you mean?"

"Whoever had plans for this project needed a golf course with extra land around it, and decided to use a little coercion."

"How do you come up with these ideas?" I asked.

"I've got a devious mind," Mack said, "comes from reading Machiavelli."

We followed a dirt road that ran around the perimeter of the course and headed for a grove of trees near the bay.

Struggling through the thick undergrowth of vines and brambles, we came upon a narrow path that sloped down towards the water.

We got to the shoreline, and I looked back at the small forest we had come through. A sign by the path read: "Private property. Trespassers will be prosecuted."

"Look at that," Mack said.

A large oak tree seemed to dominate the stand of woods.

Mack said, "Maybe there's a side path we missed." With that, he headed back into the woods.

We worked out way back more slowly, looking carefully for footprints or some other indication of a turn off, using the oak tree as a guide.

The path turned towards the golf course, and at that juncture, Mack pulled some pine branches aside. "Look," he said, "there's another path. Looks like it heads back towards the oak tree."

I was getting excited. Could this be the old "treasure oak tree?"

"Don't get carried away, Sal. If there was any treasure here, it was probably found or moved a long time ago."

"Well, you never know," I said.

When we finally go to the tree, we found that it stood in the center of a small clearing. The ground around the base had been trodden bare, as if there had been regular visitors to the site. There were beer cans in the weeds, along with matchbooks and discarded, empty cigarette packs.

Mack poked at the ashes of a small fire, saying, "Looks like this was a hangout for someone, teenagers having a party, maybe. Let's take a look at the tree."

About ten feet up the trunk, there was a hole about ten inches in diameter.

Mack said, "Hoist me up there, Sal. I want to take a closer look."

"Why me?" I grumbled, bending over.

"Well, I certainly couldn't lift you," he said, "You weigh almost twice as much as I do."

"Be careful you don't get bit by a squirrel or something," I said.

Mack grunted as he reached into the hole. "It's pretty deep," he said, "I can't see all the way to the bottom."

I let him down, not too gracefully.

He said, "Do you have a flashlight in the car?"

I went back to the car, retrieved a flashlight, and returned to the tree. We did our balancing act once again, even though my back was beginning to show signs of stress.

From above my head, Mack said, "Looks like the hole is empty all the way down." He paused, then said, "There's some kind of white powder at the bottom. Let me see if I can reach it."

By straining and extending his arm, Mack was able to come up with a pinch of white powder that looked like talcum.

Mack said, "I bet I know what this is. Do you know what cocaine tastes like?"

"No, but I'll bet if we took this to your friend Captain Hightower, he could tell us."

Chapter 27

"Golf is an open exhibition of overweening ambition, courage deflated by stupidity, skill soured by a whiff of arrogance."
—Alistair Cooke

Captain Hightower called later that week, and said, "Sal? You were right. That stuff tested out as pure, high-grade cocaine. Where did you say you found it? In the hollow of a tree? I don't believe it."

I said, "Well, it's the truth. And we have a theory as to how it got there."

Hightower said, "Theories are one thing, proof is another. Get me some evidence. Better yet, why don't you come in and outline your theories, and we'll let the real detectives take it from there?"

Ouch! There he goes with that "real detectives" routine. When were we going to be taken seriously? After all, no one ever questioned Sam Spade or Spencer.

Mack and I reviewed what we had. First, there was the death of Stanley, then the attack on Juan, then the death of Stanley's brother. Everything seemed to revolve around the golf course and the nearby water. Coincidence? Maybe. But sometimes coincidences can't be ignored. The common denominator seemed to lie at the oversized feet of Leroy Kemp. Somehow, we had to find out how he was involved in all of this.

Hope for an answer came in an invitation from Mae the following week.

When she called, she said to Mack, "You and Sal have been so helpful on the golf course. I'm sure my game is improving. To say thank you, I would like to invite you to Leroy's birthday party. He's going to be 65, you know. The party is going to be held at the country club, and I won't take 'no' for an answer."

How could we refuse the chance to get close to Leroy?

The country club where the party was to be held was located in the middle of the island, laid out along the hills that presented a view of the Sound and Great South Bay, depending on whether you were playing the front nine or the back nine. At one time, the course was a dumping ground for solid and liquid waste, and the waterholes were said to be toxic. However, that was years ago, and the bulldozers and landscapers had done their work well, covering up the environmental excesses of the past.

The road leading to the clubhouse and restaurant was lined with expensive condos and flowering trees. The parking lot was filled with Hummers, Porsches, Navigators, and Escalades. We were clearly out of our league, automotively speaking.

When we entered the club, we were greeted by Mae, who took us by the arm to greet her husband. The man of the hour was holding court by the bar, a Bourbon in one hand and a Cuban cigar in the other. He smiled broadly as we walked up. "There's the guys that have been putting up with my wife for the last few weeks. I want to thank you for keeping her out of my hair."

Mack said, "It was our pleasure, Leroy. Mae has a nice touch with the short irons, and putts like a pro."

Leroy laughed. "Well, she always was a fast learner. Look how she learned how to deal with me. We had the fastest engagement on record, and were married in a month, Las Vegas style."

The Gonzago twins stood at Leroy's side, stone-faced, unmoved by the social banter. Leroy said, "You know the Gonzago boys, Sal?"

I said, "Yeah, I remember watching you guys play football. You sure liked to hit."

The twins didn't say anything, but one of them grunted in assent.

Leroy said, "The boys used to work in our clam operation, too." It was as if he was flaunting our suspicion in our faces.

Looking directly at the twins, Mack said, "What are you guys doing these days? Going to college? Managing hedge funds?"

One of them looked befuddled, "Hedge fund? What's that?"

Mack said, "Well, both activities involve lots of money. What are you driving these days?"

It turned out that the twins both drove Hummers, not bad for someone in their twenties.

Mack said to Leroy, "Well, I guess the boys have done all right for themselves. I suppose they helped you with your campaign, too."

Leroy said, "Yes, they helped me get out the vote. Volunteered to drive shut-ins and old folks to the polls, things like that."

I could picture the twins picking up a senior citizen and driving him to the polls, applying a little persuasion, maybe intimidation along the way.

Mack said to Leroy, "Could we talk privately for a few minutes? We've heard some rumors around town, and want to tell you about them."

Leroy said, "What rumors? What are you talking about?" His face was flushed, and he looked at Mack with narrowed eyes.

He and Mack walked out on the patio overlooking the practice putting green. After a few minutes, their conversation became more animated, with Leroy waving his arms in the air. Finally, he shouted, "You're fulla shit! You don't know what you're talking about! You're gonna have to talk to my lawyer from now on."

He stormed back into the clubhouse, and at that moment, Mae signaled for the assemblage to start singing "Happy Birthday." A motley choir of expressions danced across Leroy's face as he swallowed his anger and tried to present a benign facade for his well-wishers. Occasionally, he glared at us before turning to the next person who had rushed up to shake his hand. We saw the Gonzago boys edging around the crowd, making their way towards us.

Mack said, "I think it is time for us to leave."

Chapter 28

"Golf asks something of a man. It makes one loathe mediocrity." —*Gary Player*

A week later, I got a threat in the mail. It was the typical threat, with the letters of the message cut and pasted from magazines and newspapers. It read:

"Stop sticking your nose where it don't belong. We know where your grandchildren live."

I believe I mentioned once the new arrangement my former wife Carol and I have. While we do not live together (yet, I hope soon), we have joint custody of our deceased daughter's children. Carol takes care of them most of the time, and when she is attending class at the local community college, they attend the day care program offered by the same school. I usually see the children in the evenings and on weekends, time that Carol and I agreed on earlier to try to restore our relationship. Life gets complicated sometimes. But somehow caring for the children has brought us even closer together, even in our later years. There is no room for anyone else in my small, bachelor's apartment, so the children stay with Carol in the house we lived in when we were married.

This threat was not something we could take lightly. I drove over to the college, situated on the grounds of a former tuberculosis sanitarium overlooking Long Island Sound. I waited for Carol outside her building, and when she came out of the door, chattering away with some young classmates, my heart gave a sudden leap. I saw the same girl I had fallen in love with many years ago, unchanged by time and travail. She saw me and waved.

In the college cafeteria, we sat down over cups of coffee, and I showed her the letter. She paled, then said, "Oh, Sal, this is awful. What are we going to do?"

"I don't know. One thing for sure, it's the kind of threat we need to take to the police. Maybe get some kind of protection, though I wouldn't expect much from our overworked force at this time of year."

"Well, we need to do something. First off, you need to move back into our house. I've been meaning to suggest that anyway. The kids miss you when you're not there, and I- I…"

I reached out for her hand, and said, "I know what you're saying, and I feel the same way. I'll bring my stuff over tonight."

She smiled, even though there was a tear in her eye, and said, "Just leave the cigars in your apartment, O.K.?"

"All right, but before I come over, I'm going to take this note over to the police department. They know what we've been working on, and Mack has a good idea where this threat probably came from."

When I went to the police department later that day, I had the misfortune to run into our friend, Lieutenant Fagan. He was not encouraging. He said, "Ah, it's probably a prank by some kids, maybe your old students. I wouldn't worry about it."

I said, "That may be, sir, but I would appreciate it if you would make a copy of this for me and show the original to Captain Hightower."

He grumbled, "We got more things to do than worry about some nut prank of yours."

I said, "Fagan, I'm a taxpayer, and I want to remind you that you work for me. If you won't show this to Hightower, I will personally see that he gets it, and let him know how helpful you have been."

"All right, all right, don't get your shorts in a wringer. I'll take care of it."

"Fine, but let me have that copy."

After my interview with Fagan, I stopped by Mack's place. He was sitting at the computer in his garage, and said, "Wait, Sal, I'll be right with you. I just want to finish this up."

"What are you working on?"

"I'm making a time line of everything we have come up with since Stanley's death. There are some interesting anomalies."

"Well, here's another anomaly for you," I said, as I showed him the copy of the threat.

He looked at it closely, then said, "That's a nasty piece of business. And we know where it came from, don't we?"

He thought for a moment, then said, "What are we going to do?"

I found the "we" reassuring, but was not surprised, because that's the way Mack is.

"First thing I'm doing is move back into the house with Carol and the kids. Having me around will offer some security for her, and for me."

"Yes, you're right, and it's about time you and Carol stopped beating around the bush. It's always been clear that you two belong together anyway. But I have a feeling that this is only a stopgap measure. We may have to think long-range here."

"Maybe we should send them down to the ranch in Florida, too."

"I'm not sure that would be fair to Dan and Belle. But Carol's parents live over in Daytona Beach, don't they?"

"Let me give Dan a call. Maybe we could put Carol and the kids on the train to Sanford, and he could take them over to Daytona Beach."

And so it was that our loved ones wound up in the Sunshine State, while we two middle-aged warriors got ready for the battle of our lives.

Meanwhile, Mack got an invitation.

Chapter 29

"Golf is not a game of great shots. It is a game of the most misses. The people who win make the smallest mistakes." —Gene Littler

The invitation came from the United States Golf Association in Far Hills, New Jersey, and we were being asked to serve as stewards at the upcoming U.S. Open at Shinnecock Hills, one of the oldest courses in the country.

In 1891 to be exact the sport known as golf came to Long Island, and subsequently the rest of the United States, when a Scottish-Canadian golfer was commissioned to design a twelve-hole course on the rolling Shinnecock Hills, which lie between the two ridges that form the backbone of the island. The site was picked because it resembled the terrain of the coastal lowlands of Scotland, where the sport was already popular. Using 150 Native Americans from the nearby reservation, the course was built almost entirely by hand. Some Indian burial mounds were left intact for religious reasons, and eventually became bunkers for sand traps, a kind of unwitting revenge on the white conquerors. Thus Shinnecock Hills became the first golf club on Long Island, and one of the first in the United States. It was the site of the 1896 and 1986 Open Tournaments. No Native Americans were invited to play in either tournament. However, a few of the descendants of the original builders were allowed to caddy.

Today there are over 100 public and private golf courses on Long Island, covering an area of over 100,000 acres, larger than the principalities of Lichtenstein and Monaco combined. Each year, what was once a thriving potato industry gives way to housing developments, and more golf courses.

When we learned that the latest U.S. Open was going to be played on Long Island, Mack and I, as members of the local volunteer fire department, had heard that the organizers of the Open were looking for first responders to serve as stewards. It was a natural fit, as many firefighters, who are also trained in CPR and other emergency procedures, are known to be avid golfers. Every year, there are at least 50 department-sponsored tournaments on the island, usually intended to raise money for the firemen's benevolent fund. We entered our name in the department drawing, as they were taking only two or three members from each of the 90-odd departments on the island. I guess we got lucky.

As more than 50,000 spectators, volunteers, and corporate guests descended on Shinnecock Hills by train and car, they would be met by officials wielding metal detectors, a six-foot fence surrounding the club house, a National Guard Weapons of Mass Destruction Team, and bomb-sniffing dogs.

In addition, a small army of agencies would be on hand to assist the local police force and fire department, including the State Police, the County Police, the Sheriff's Department, the FBI, and the U.S. Postal Service, which was prepared to oversee package deliveries. Also, the Air National Guard, the Bay Constables, and the Coast Guard were on alert. Four emergency medical care sites had been established on the course, and emergency medical technicians on bicycles and golf carts would be carrying defibrillators. Clearly, the U.S. Open would be ready for any eventuality.

Joining us were a host of other volunteers who would help to keep order at the tournament. Mack and I were assigned to the 17th hole, where we would be joined by Chief Don Gackenheimer and Tom Kost from the Suffolk County Fire Academy. The hole was dedicated to the memory of Fire Academy instructor and FDNY firefighter Ray Meisenheimer, who lost his life on 9/11.

There was a long list of items that spectators were not allowed to bring to the tournament: cell phones, packages, food, drinks, television sets, radios, coolers, animals (other than seeing eye dogs—though why one would want a seeing eye dog at a golf tournament is beyond me.), bicycles, chairs, ladders, signs, banners, or metal spike shoes.

The biggest problem would be protecting spectators from themselves. When you get a lot of older, out-of-shape people walking four or five miles in 90-degree heat, not hydrating to compensate, you have a medical emergency. There would also be a number of cases of tick bites and Lyme disease.

When we weren't keeping an eye on the spectators, we might catch a glimpse of some of the best golfers in the world.

First, we had to find a safe haven for Carol and my grandchildren. We called Dan Laybourne, and after I explained our situation, his response was not surprising. "Hey, bring them all down here. The more the merrier. Juan has been a great help, what a fantastic kid. We got most of the damage from the last hurricane cleared up, and he's learning to ride."

I said, "Dan, I appreciate your generous offer. But that's a lot of mouths to feed, and the kids are kind of young. You and Belle don't want to start changing diapers at your age. Besides, Carol has already spoken to her folks over in Daytona Beach. Could you meet Carol and the kids at Sanford and drive them over there?"

"Sure, pal, no problem. But when are you and Mack coming down?"

I told him about our invitation to the U.S. Open, and brought him up to date on our investigation.

He said, "You guys must be getting pretty close, getting threats like that. Be careful. You're not young bucks anymore, you know."

Chapter 30

"America is one vast golf course these days."
—The Duke of Windsor

The United States Golf Association Open was upon us before we knew it. Buses carried fans from a nearby airport, and others came by train. By the thousands, they poured through the gates, stopped briefly by security checks. There was a large bin full of cell phones, confiscated from people who had not read the rules. Like maddened lemmings, the fans swarmed from hole to hole, trying to get a sight of their favorite golfer. Some had the good sense to pick a hole, establish a viewing spot, and wait for the golfers to come to them.

The weather was perfect for golf: warm, but not too hot. A gentle breeze blew in from the ocean. It would be warmer later in the day, and the beer concessions would do a booming business, adding to the potential dehydration of the overweight walkers.

Mack and I took our assigned positions on either side of the 17th tee. Our job was to hold a rope and keep the fans off the tee. At times, depending on the popularity of the golfer, the crowd would push against the line, as if mere proximity to him would improve their game. We held the line tightly, not giving way. The head steward held a sign indicating when the fans were to be quiet while the golfer addressed his ball.

The Tiger was about to hit one of his patented 300-yard drives before a hushed crowd. I couldn't keep my eyes away from one of the most famous players in the world, so I turned away from the crowd to watch him. As I looked across the tee, my gaze went to the other side, where Mack was stationed. He was watching Tiger too, as was almost everybody within shouting distance. Suddenly, I saw one of the Gonzago twins working his way through the crowd behind Mack. Before I could call out a warning, the Tiger hit a towering drive, and my shout of alarm was drowned out by cries of encouragement from the crowd: "In the hole! Go get 'em, Tiger!"

Mack suddenly fell to the ground, clutching at his back. At the same time, I heard a commotion behind me. I turned around and saw the other Gonzago twin struggling and cursing, each arm held tightly by Chiefs Whittam and Kost from the fire academy. Chief Gackenheimer held a plastic tent stake.

Gackenheimer said, "This bozo was sneaking up behind you, Sal, with this thing in his hand." I looked at the stake. It was the kind of implement that could be bought at any sporting goods store, and was the type used to hold down the corporate sponsor's and concession tents that ringed the course. The stake had been sharpened to a fine point, and had become a lethal weapon.

I said, "Thanks, Don, hold on to him, will you?"

I rushed across the tee area, now empty since the players and crowd had moved on to the next hole. A few stragglers looked at our little drama, watching it play out. Mack was lying on the ground, moaning and writhing in pain. A couple of emergency medical technicians appeared, and immediately began administering first aid. A stretcher was nearby, on the back of an all-terrain vehicle rigged as an emergency carrier. Having stabilized Mack, the emergency medical technicians were about to put him on it when an ambulance approached on a service road, followed by a couple of police cars.

"Where's the other twin?" I thought, as Mack was being loaded into the ambulance.

I looked across the course, and thought I saw someone muscling his way through the fans, away from the action, against the flow of the crowd. Yes, it was the other twin! I grabbed the arm of one of the police officers, and said, "There's the guy who stabbed Mack!"

We set off in the direction of the fleeing felon, who was running in the direction of the bay. The cop said, "We've got him now. He's headed right for the water."

As we approached the bay, I saw the twin jump into a Boston Whaler that had been tied up near the shore, disguised by reeds and underbrush.

The cop grabbed his walkie-talkie and called security control, saying, "The suspect is getting away by boat. Call the Coast Guard! He's in a Boston Whaler."

The whaler headed out into open water, only to be cut off by a police boat. The twin Evinrudes on the police boat overhauled the whaler with ease, and an officer with a bull horn warned the twin to cut power or be fired upon. At that moment, a Coast Guard boat appeared on the scene.

The fleeing Gonzago twin didn't have a chance.

Chapter 31

Once in custody, the twins sang like a pair of blue birds, trying to save themselves.

Our friend Captain Hightower showed us a copy of their interview, which read in part:

Question: "What are your names?"

Answer: "Eric Gonzago."

"Anthony Gonzago."

Question: "O.K. since we have the testimony of Sal Cascio and a couple of other witnesses, why don't you tell us why you attacked him and Mr. Thomas?"

Eric said, "Because they were getting too close."

Anthony blurted out, "Don't say anything, fool! Remember, we don't say anything, just ask for a lawyer."

Interviewer: "Who told you that?"

Eric: "I don't care. It wasn't our fault. We were just following orders, to protect ourselves."

Interviewer: "What do you mean?"

Eric: "Mr. Kemp said that if we said anything, we would wind up like Old Stanley."

Interviewer: "Mr. Kemp? You mean Coach Kemp?"

Eric: "Yeah. He said if we gave up the drug operation, the Colombians would be after us and our families."

It turns out, as we had suspected, that they had been ordered by

Leroy Kemp to get rid of us, just as they had dispatched Stanley and his brother, because we were getting too close to the truth. Because of his political aspirations, Kemp was desperate to distance himself from the clamming/drug operation, part of a larger scheme set up by a Colombian cartel.

He knew we were getting close because Detective Fagan, who was on his payroll, had been keeping him informed.

Fagan was on another payroll: the Colombian drug cartel that was trying to put some of its ill-gotten gains into a legitimate business, the Treasure Oak golf course and condominium complex.

Mack said, "Now we know who was trying to scare the Japanese off. It wasn't a matter of racism or old World War II wounds, it was just a matter of business."

I said, "Yeah, like the old days of the Mafia, when the five families of the New York area moved their money into legal enterprises like waste removal and restaurant supplies."

Captain Hightower showed us the interview with Fagan, who was suspended from the force until the investigation was completed.

Captain Hightower: "You know you have been named as part of the Kemp scheme. The Gonzago twins said you passed Kemp's directives on to them, and you told them what we were finding out from Cascio and Thomas. What else should we know about?"

Fagan said, "If I tell you every thing, that I'm just a middle man, will I have a chance at a lesser sentence?"

Hightower: "Yeah, I'll do what I can for you. Up to know, you had a pretty good record. Why did you get involved with these dirt bags, Alfonse?"

Fagan said, "Well, you know I have a couple of kids in college and a sick wife. The house is mortgaged to the hilt, and I had a tough time making monthly expenses. Basically, I needed the dough, and Leroy needed someone on the inside."

"So what can you tell us about Leroy's involvement with the Treasure Oak?"

Fagan said, "The Colombians were pressuring Leroy to find a legitimate outlet for their money. Land on a place like Long Island is a pretty good investment, even if there has been a sag in real estate lately. Golf courses are booming. Like fire departments, they're pretty much not affected by recessions."

Hightower asked, "What about those attacks on the Japanese golfers?"

Fagan said, "I knew that Jimmy Mattas hated the Japanese. I also knew that he was a whiz when it came to making realistic-looking model airplanes. He needed money, too, so I hired him to rig some planes for the attacks. We also messed up one of their greens with a message. I think they got the point."

Chapter 32

"The difference between golf and government is that in golf you can't improve your lie." —George Deukmejian

Fortunately, the emergency medical technicians treating Mack knew their stuff. They applied continuous pressure on the wound to control the bleeding. As soon as he was loaded into the ambulance, they started an IV drip.

By the time I got to the hospital, he had been stabilized and given a booster tetanus shot. I met Dr. Bill Roche, the emergency room doctor, just outside Mack's room, and he brought me up to date on the patient's condition.

"Sal, I think he's going to be all right. The stab wound is on the right side of his back, but not life-threatening. The implement, what was it, a tent stake, they said? Well, it went through his skin and the subcutaneous tissue, and that's where Mack got lucky. If the stake had continued on its path, it would have pierced the pleural cavity, the lung, and the wound could have been fatal. However, the stake slid off one of his ribs, maybe when he reacted to being stabbed, and did only muscular damage. There was hemorrhage and bruising along the wound path."

"So he's going to be O.K.?"

"Yes. He won't want to swing a golf club for a few weeks, but barring any infection, I think he'll be back to his ornery self before you know it."

I went into Mack's room. He was lying on his stomach, sipping a cup of ice water through a straw. He had a loopy grin on his face, probably from the painkillers.

He said, "Hey, partner. I hear we got them."

"Yeah, but you should have been paying attention to the crowd."

"I know, I know. But I couldn't resist watching Tiger's drive. How many times to you get to see him up close like that?"

He thought for a moment, then said, "I guess we're not going to be playing golf for a few weeks. Maybe we should take a vacation, go down to Florida and join the ladies."

"Let me check with the doc and find out how soon you can travel."

Two weeks later, we boarded a Southwest Airlines plane at MacArthur Airport, non-stop to Orlando. Dan picked us up, and that night we were sitting down to dinner and beers at our favorite fish camp, the Hungry Gator. Mack still moved a bit stiffly, like an old man, and Maria hovered over him like a mother cat. At first, she was angry with both of us.

"You are too old to be playing detectives," she said. "Leave the crime solving to the young men, the young police."

Later in her tirade, I noticed a touch of pride mixed in with the fear. "So now Juan can go back to school without worrying about bad people attacking him. He will like that."

The next morning, I borrowed one of the Laybourne cars and drove over to Daytona Beach to see Carol and the twins. That night, we sat down to what I hoped would be a romantic dinner in a Thai restaurant. Carol listened with horrified fascination while I recounted the twisted story of Leroy Kemp and his nefarious underlings.

Finally, she said, "Why, they're just a bunch of modern-day smugglers! What will happen to them?"

"Well, the Gonzago twins have been charged with assault and attempted murder. Mack will go back north to testify when they go to trial."

"What about Kemp? You know, I never did like that man."

"His case is a little more complicated. He quickly hired a high-priced lawyer, and a lot of the evidence is hearsay and circumstantial.

His political career is ruined, since his name was all over the newspapers when he was arrested. Of course, he had to resign from the school board. And his wife is filing for divorce. I guess he's got a slew of problems, including his Colombian associates."

Carol said, "I'm so proud of you and Mack. But you took a big chance."

"I know, I know. Maria said the same thing. Next you're going to tell me that I'm too old to be a detective."

"No, Sal, you're never going to be too old for that….and other things."

We pursued those "other things" later that night, and I am glad to say that I wasn't too old for that, either.

The next morning, we were eating breakfast when the telephone rang. Carol's Dad answered, and handed the phone to me. It was Mack.

"Hey, partner. How's everything over there?"

"Just fine. What's up?"

"We were sitting around, talking about things to do. I suggested Disney World, thinking that Juan would enjoy it. Turns out that Dan and Belle took him there last week. Anyway, I've got an urge for Cuban food and margaritas. What do you and Carol say to a weekend in Key West?"

Carol's parents said they would love to take care of their grandchildren for another week, so we headed back towards Orlando to pick up Mack and Maria. Juan volunteered to take care of the horses and the other animals at the ranch so Dan and Belle could join us on our jaunt to Key West. We piled into Dan's Escalade and headed south.

Chapter 33

"One of the most fascinating things about golf is how it reflects the cycle of life. No matter what you shoot, the next day you have to go back to the first tee and begin all over again and make yourself into something." —Peter Jacobsen

As we took the long ride on U.S. 1, I thought about Key West, Cayo Hueso, the Island of Bones. Having been there once before, I was reminded that Key West reveals its beauty slowly. Driving into Old Town, I felt the soft breezes coming in from the Gulf. Tanned bicyclists appeared on either side of us, like dolphins leading a boat to shore. Faded houseboats nestled against the seawall, and windsurfers skittered across the waves in the distance. Nomads from as far away as Canada and Kansas swapped lies in tubular aluminum folding chairs in front of battered Air Stream trailers. Tropical flowers grew wild in vacant lots between high-rise condos. Roosters crowed in back alleys, defending their turf.

We checked into the Ocean House, located at the foot of Duval Street. Duval is a glossy old queen, lined with T-shirt shops managed by Israelis and Syrians, living and working side-by-side in peaceful competition. There were porn shops next to fashionable boutiques, art galleries and shops selling the ubiquitous postcards: the Hemingway House, the Audobon House, and bare-breasted bathing beauties. Homeless teenagers braided hair, slept, and begged from the steps of the Episcopal Church. Key West is a lurid fantasy town, with its vine-covered cottages, bike-drawn rickshaws, tea dances, lime-green fire trucks, and pink taxi cabs. It is the last place, the last stop on U.S. 1, the place of escape from which there is no escape, except the colorful cemetery in the center of town, where tourists come to read the quaint sayings on the tombstones: "I told you I was sick," and "At least I know where he's sleeping tonight."

As we drove down Duval Street, we saw a banner stretched across the way, reading,

"Welcome to the Pirates in Paradise Festival!"

Mack looked at me and said, "That's spooky. Seems we are being haunted by pirates these days. Think the ghost of Blackbeard has followed us down here?"

After dinner at El Meson de Pepe, we joined Captain Finbar and his scurvy crew of pirates aboard the schooner Wolf, flagship of the Conch Republic, for a sunset sail, hoping to catch a flash of green as the sun sank in the west.

The next day, we went to Fort Zachary Taylor to visit the Village Thieves' Market and Pirate Fest. "Pirates" repelled invaders along the ramparts of the fort while vendors sold their wares in the makeshift town. Occasional fights broke out, with braggarts solving their disagreements with swords and daggers in true pirate style. Spirited sea chanteys resounded from the taverns.

Mack, ever the history teacher, filled us in on the background of Key West. He said, "At one time Key West was one of the wealthiest cities in America. How did they get their money? By luring ships with signal fires and giving bad advice on routes, the nefarious wreckers would entice ships into grounding themselves on the treacherous reefs and shoals that surround the island. Hundreds of ships were lost. Most of the time, the crews were saved, but oddly the cargo was lost, only to show up in someone's warehouse on the island. And of course, there's Mel Fisher."

"Who's he? Another pirate?" Carol asked.

"Well, on September 10, 1622, a twenty-eight ship convoy left Havana headed for Spain, loaded to the gun whales with treasure from South and Central America. A two-day hurricane ended for eight of the ships any hope of making it home. Among these were the *Santa Margarita* and the *Nuesta Senora de Atocha*. Mel Fisher never stopped thinking about the Atocha as he and his crew searched for over 12 years for her last resting place. After years of fruitless searching, unfortunate deaths, and horrible accidents, Fisher and his crew hit pay dirt. In 1985, they found the Atocha, along with nearly 1,000 bars of silver and an incredible treasure of gold and jewels. Since that discovery, Key West has become a destination for a whole new generation of treasure hunters."

As we drove back to the hotel, Maria said, "I think we have had enough of pirates and buried treasure. Let's go home."

Chapter 34

When we got off the plane at MacArthur Airport, we were met by our friend Captain Hightower, who had a worried look on his face.

Mack said, "What's up, John?"

Hightower took us aside, and said, "I don't want to disturb the ladies, but you fellas should know that the Gonzago twins made bail."

"How can that be?" I asked. "We caught them red-handed."

Mack said, "Yeah, they weren't playing golf at the Open, they were playing for blood."

Hightower responded, "Well, that may be, but this is still the United States, where you are innocent until proven guilty. The arrests were made pretty much on your testimony. No one actually saw a Gonzago stab Mack, and while the other one was approaching you with a sharpened stake in his hand, no one actually can say what he was going to do with it. Intent is not grounds for jail time, without your testimony at the hearing."

Mack said, "So where are these guys now? Has anyone been keeping track of them?"

Hightower said, "Not too closely. We don't have the manpower for that. That's why I'm warning you. Watch your backs, and lock your doors at night. And if I were you, I would put an alarm system in your houses."

Mack already had a system, and I decided I had better do the same.

I said, "Thanks for letting us know, John. We'll keep an eye out for them."

The next month was uneventful. We settled back into our individual routines: Maria went back to work, Juan enrolled in a couple of courses at the community college, and Carol had her hands full with our grandchildren. Mack and I worked our usual cases in the daytime: insurance fraud, theft of cable service, and even a juicy divorce. As the days passed, we were lulled into a sense of false security, it turns out.

We did not realize it until we decided to go sailing.

Now, I am not a big fan of sailing. In fact, I prefer a "stink pot," a motor boat that gets me from the dock to the beach on Fire Island in the quickest and most efficient manner. Mack, on the other hand, grew up in a sailing family, and was racing Blue Jays when he was ten or twelve.

Mack was the proud owner of a cat boat, a type of sail boat known for its simplicity of design, ease of handling, shallow draft, and large capacity. Mack called it his "old man's boat," because it was so easy to handle. The single-sail boat wasn't very fast, but it was safe, and could carry a number of people across the bay.

On a bright, sunny, spring afternoon, Mack, Maria, Juan, and I set out for a sail across the bay. Our destination was the old Coast Guard station on Fire Island, which had a lovely beach. Maria was a little nervous, for this was her first time on a sailboat, and as she confessed, she didn't swim very well. Sailing was new to Juan, too, but fortunately he was a strong swimmer.

A strong wind blew from the southwest, and the boat was handling so well that Mack decided to sail farther east, towards Moriches Inlet.

Shouting over the wind, I said, "You're not going too close to the inlet, are you? The tide is going out, you know."

Mack said, "Don't worry. I won't go too close. I'm about to come about pretty soon, and we can tack over to the Coast Guard station."

I said, "Well, don't wait too long. Otherwise, we'll be sailing home in the dark."

Mack laughed, saying, "Well, I sort of figured on a romantic moonlight sail with my honey here." With that, he smiled at Maria, who laughed nervously.

At that moment, a couple of sleek motorboats appeared. One was the notorious cigarette boat, known for its speed and maneuverability. We could not see who was operating them at first, since they threw up so much spray. The boats started circling us, like sharks closing in on a hapless swimmer. Suddenly, there was the chatter of what sounded like a submachine gun, and a line of holes stitched their way across the sail. We all ducked below the gunwhale, as another burst chewed its way through the single mast of our boat.

I looked up over the side, and saw one of the Gonzago twins laughing maniacally. Then, as quickly as they had appeared, the boats raced away.

As we drifted towards the Moriches Inlet, we were propelled by the wind from the west.

Mack had a worried look on his face. All we had was a rudder, and we were moving towards the inlet faster and faster.

Mack said, "The tide is going to carry us out into the ocean!"

We could see beyond the inlet, where giant waves crashed onto the barrier island. Our 20-foot cat boat wouldn't stand a chance of survival.

Mack shouted, "I'm going to try to steer us close to the breakwater." He pointed to huge piles of stones placed by the Army Corps of Engineers to keep the inlet open.

As we sped through the inlet, Mack worked the rudder back and forth, trying to get us closer to the nearest breakwater. He shouted to Juan, "Son, grab our mooring line, there, the rope by the bow. When I give the word, see if you can swim with the rope to the rocks. See that flag pole towards the end of the breakwater? That's our only chance."

Juan nodded, a grim but determined look on his face. We got closer and closer to the breakwater, and closer to the outlet to the raging ocean. Mack yelled to Juan, and at his signal, Juan leaped overboard, the rope wrapped around his arm. With strong, sure strokes, he swam towards the rocks.

We watched with held breath as he reached the rocks, climbed up to the flag pole, and secured the rope.

The plan worked. The bowline held, swinging us toward the end of the breakwater. I grabbed the line and pulled myself in, joining Juan. Together, we pulled on the line, working the boat in close enough so that Maria and Mack could disembark. Just as they joined us on the breakwater, the rope snapped, probably frayed by the sharp edge of a rock. We watched in horrified fascination as the boat hit the giant breakers. It flipped in the air, and was consumed by the waves.

Some campers near the inlet came rushing up to our aid, and soon we were sitting in front of a trailer, comforted with blankets and hot cups of coffee. The camper, a New York cop named Don, was calling the Suffolk County Police on his cell phone.

In about twenty minutes, a Suffolk County Police helicopter landed at the campsite, and we were airlifted to police headquarters, where we were met by Chief Hightower.

"I told you guys to be careful, so what do you do? Go sailing?"

Mack grinned sheepishly, saying, "It's my fault, Chief. Things got so quiet, I thought we would be all right."

The Chief said, "Well, as old school teachers you should know. When things get quiet, something's going to happen. And it has, in this case. It looks like the Gonzago boys have left town. they missed their first court appearance."

Mack said, "Now we have another attempted murder charge against them, because Sal said he saw one of them in the boats that attacked us."

Hightower said, "Well, we suspected they would run. Their trucks are impounded, and we have been watching the train stations."

Mack said, "I wonder where they got those high-powered boats from, and who was on the boat with them?"

Hightower said, "Probably Leroy Kemp's Colombian 'associates.' We believe they put up the bail money for the Gonzagos, but can't prove it."

I said, "Looks like a job for Dom Evangelista."

Mack said, "Dom who?"

I said, "You probably don't remember him. He never made it to your Advanced Placement History class."

When Dominick Evangelista was in high school, he was, in his own words, "a holy terror," headed for an early drop out and eventually jail. But as is the case so often, a couple of teachers took an interest in him, and turned him around. He said to me once, "I owe a debt of gratitude to Richard Hawkey and you, Coach, for keeping me in line. You never punished me, but always explained the consequences of my behavior. You showed that you believed in me."

After high school and work as a store detective, Dominick became a bounty hunter, or as he prefers to be called, a "fugitive recovery agent."

In his dangerous line of work, Dominick has been stabbed twice in the line of duty and has had to duck his share of bullets. However, he prefers to use his wits and psychology to get a defendant to honor the terms of his bail agreement. When all else fails, he uses pepper spray or a stun gun.

It sounds like dangerous work, but sometimes the payoff is worth it. When he recovers a fugitive, Dominick gets up to 20 percent of the bail amount, which can add up to the thousands.

If anyone could track the Gonzago twins, it would be Dominick Evangelista.

Epilogue

A couple of weeks later, I got an e-mail from Dom Evangelista. It read: "Greetings from sunny Florida. I apprehended the brothers in Miami, about to board a plane for Colombia. Had to use my stun gun, sorry to say, but they refused to give up without a struggle. My partner and I are on our way back to Long Island, with the fugitives chained to the floor in my van. Will let you know when the court date is re-assigned. Cheers, Dom."

"Well, good for him," I said out loud.

"Good for who?" said Mack, who was looking at a book.

"I just heard from Dom Evangelista. He caught the Gonzago boys, and is bringing them back to Long Island for trial."

"Good for him! Another Cascio student success story!"

"Well, he did turn out O.K. didn't he?"

I couldn't blame Mack for being a little preoccupied, for he and Maria were planning a wedding. What he didn't know yet was that it was to be a double wedding, for Carol and I had decided to give it another try.

After all, as Thornton Wilder said in *Our Town*, "People are meant to live two by two in this world," and we planned to prove the truth of that statement.

That night, Carol and I were walking along the beach after a dinner at La Margherita, our favorite restaurant. The moon was up, glistening across the bay. There was a soft breeze that ruffled Carol's still golden hair. As we walked, I kicked something shiny in the sand. I stooped to pick it up. It was heavy and felt like a brass token. When we got home, I examined my find more closely.

It was a gold doubloon.

CPSIA information can be obtained at www.ICGtesting.com
Printed in the USA
LVOW09s1902090215

426300LV00001B/327/P